"Can I beg you
to stick around
said. **"Help me**

"I don't think so."

She put her hand on the door, intending to climb out, but he leaned across and stopped her, laying one arm across both of hers. She froze. His bare arm brushed her stomach and would brush her breasts if she leaned just a little bit.

At one time they'd been way more intimate with each other than this, so she shouldn't feel uncomfortable about it. Problem was, his touch opened up too many memories, and too many lost possibilities.

"I'm not joking, okay?" he said, with his voice dropped low. "Stay. A couple of weeks."

"I—I can't."

"You're on school summer break. Your family can manage without you. Some people consider Stoneport a great place for a vacation."

Her heart shouldn't race like this. Her head shouldn't spin. And she should absolutely not consider that he was offering a second chance at their marriage.

Lilian Darcy is Australian, but has strong ties to the USA through her American husband. They have four growing children, and currently live in Canberra, Australia. Lilian has written over fifty romance novels, many for the Mills & Boon® Medical Romance™ series, and still has more story ideas crowding into her head than she knows what to do with. Her work has appeared on romance bestseller lists, and two of her plays have been nominated for major Australian writing awards. 'I'll keep writing as long as people keep reading my books,' she says. 'It's all I've ever wanted to do, and I love it.'

Recent titles by the same author:

Mills & Boon® Medical Romance™

THE DOCTOR'S FIRE RESCUE
THE LIFE-SAVER
PREGNANT WITH HIS CHILD
   (part of the *Crocodile Creek* mini-series)

THE MILLIONAIRE'S CINDERELLA WIFE

BY
LILIAN DARCY

MILLS & BOON®

First published in Great Britain 2006
Harlequin Mills & Boon Limited,
Eton House, 18-24 Paradise Road, Richmond, Surrey TW9 1SR

© Lilian Darcy 2006

ISBN-13: 978 0 263 84909 7
ISBN-10:   0 263 84909 0

Set in Times Roman 12½ on 15½ pt.
02-0706-48011

Printed and bound in Spain
by Litografia Rosés, S.A., Barcelona

Chapter One

At seven on a Tuesday morning in June, both the waterfront and the adjacent marina in Stoneport, North Carolina were quiet.

Pre-dawn fishing expeditions must already have departed, while the more tourist-oriented charter trips and sailing classes didn't get under way until a little later. Sierra Taylor walked from her nearby hotel, passed a café called *Tides,* open for breakfast, and decided she'd go back there and wait over coffee if the office at Garrett Marine was unattended at this hour.

On edge about the coming confrontation with Ty, she almost hoped it would be.

No such luck, she soon discovered.

Ty Garrett had always been an early riser, which must have been an asset in his business success. Through the glass door she saw a woman behind the main desk frowning at a computer screen, and when Sierra dipped the handle the door swung inward, jangling a nautical bell.

"Good morning!" The woman was young, twenty-two at most, and her voice sounded impossibly perky at this hour. Behind her head, a blonde ponytail swung through the hole in her baseball cap, keeping time to the music of her words. "Can I help you?"

"I'm here to see Mr. Garrett."

"Are you booking a sailing class? Already booked? Questions about our boat rentals? Give me your name, and—"

"Actually, no, it's personal."

"Well, give me your name…" This time she enunciated slowly and clearly, as if she dealt with too many people who weren't all that bright.

"Sierra." No point in fighting over it.

"Last name?"

"He doesn't need my last name."

"O-kay." Miss Perky Ponytail shrugged and

sashayed off down a short, dark corridor in the direction of a closed door.

She moved as if she was climbing around the deck of a sail-boat on a sunny day, and she didn't knock at the door—which must surely lead to Ty's private office—but peeled off into another room, from which Sierra soon heard various clinking and gushing sounds which suggested that coffee was being made.

She took a couple of careful breaths, reining in emotions that were too strong and too complex to fully make sense after so long. Why so much ambivalence? Why shouldn't this be easy? She'd driven the six hundred miles from Landerville, Ohio, primed for this moment and coolly determined. She really hadn't expected to feel so messed up about it.

Trying to center herself, Sierra leaned her elbow on the high desk. Her gaze idly wander over the desk's surface, taking in a pile of glossy printed brochures, a pen and a box of mints. And then she saw it—the magazine that had brought her to Stoneport—right there at an angle in front of her.

Ty's face grinned up at her from *A-list*'s front cover—tanned, sheened with sun screen and faintly dusted with salt, handsome as a Greek god. His dark hair begged for a woman's fingers to tidy its wind-swept waves. Behind him, a brightly colored spinnaker sail bellied against the breeze, while the glimpse of a sun-bronzed shoulder at the bottom of the frame strongly suggested he was shirtless.

Even though she'd seen it countless times now, the image and the four words that captioned it in bold red letters still made Sierra catch her breath with shock and self-doubt, a healthy dose of anger, and something else that she didn't want to put a name to.

"Bachelor Of The Year!" trumpeted *A-list*'s banner headline.

As for the three-page feature article inside, Sierra knew it almost by heart.

It catalogued Ty's business success here on the Stoneport waterfront. It painted in dramatic colors the story of how he'd rescued a young couple from a stricken sail-boat during a spring storm, how he'd kept the unconscious husband alive, delivered the wife's premature baby, and saved both mother and child. It quoted local residents and Garrett Marine staff praising him in extravagant terms, and guess-timated his growing wealth in the tens of millions.

Finally, just in case the front cover had left any

woman in America in any doubt, it included several more photos that proved his good looks and stunning physique were not merely the products of clever lighting and heavy use of an air-brush.

You'd have to be pretty mean-spirited to suggest that Ty Garrett hadn't earned the Bachelor of the Year label.

Sierra had only one small problem with it, herself.

She was already married to him.

Miss Ponytail had made the coffee. With a big, milkless mug of it in her hand, she finally reached the closed door and knocked. Then, without waiting for an answer, she called, "There's another one, Ty."

Sierra heard his still-familiar voice through the door. "Early bird."

"Says the worm."

"Yeah, already squirming. Does she want a class or a charter?"

Miss Ponytail opened the door a crack, leaned in and dropped her voice, but didn't drop it low enough. "No, she's going with the 'It's personal' angle. Won't give her last name. Thinks that's an original game plan, just like the other forty-seven women who have tried it."

"And is she pretty?"

"You be the judge."

"So what's the first name?"

"Sierra."

Thick silence.

Sierra discovered she'd stopped breathing.

"Here's your coffee, by the way… Oops!" Miss Ponytail said.

Appearing in the doorway, Ty had almost made her spill it, but they both recovered in time. He didn't take the hot beverage, however. Instead, his gaze arrowed over Miss Ponytail's head and reached Sierra. Lord, in the flesh he was better looking even than in the professional photos, she realized at once, as she took in a long, slow drag of air. Better than all of her memories.

He wore a white polo-neck shirt that set off his tan the way whipped cream set off chocolate mousse, and baggy navy shorts that ended just at the hard knots of muscle above his knees, and he looked at her as if he'd half-expected her but didn't fully believe she was here, all the same.

"Sierra," he said.

"Got it in one." Her tone came out flip and unnatural.

The tension in the room sang like wind through a sailboat's metal stays.

"You haven't changed so much in eight years." His guarded expression didn't telegraph his opinion on any of the changes that had occurred.

"You have, Ty," Sierra blurted out.

He'd filled out his strong frame over the past few years, and success and maturity had given him a confidence of bearing that made his jaw look as strong as iron and his blue eyes as steady as the moon. And as Sierra knew very well, he hadn't ever lacked confidence, even in his early twenties.

"I guess this one was right," Miss Ponytail said. "You really didn't need her last name."

"Cookie, can you go check that *Footloose* is ready to roll for that two-day charter?" Ty asked, not looking at Miss Ponytail.

His eyes seemed to have the power to heat Sierra's skin like a radiant lamp, and, oh, she suddenly remembered in such vivid, physical detail all the reasons why she'd once loved him so much, why she'd believed so completely in what they had, why she'd ached and burned so hard when it had ended.

"You might have to handle things on your own,

this morning," he told his employee. "And can you dump the coffee?" he added.

"Sure," Miss Ponytail said. Cookie, apparently.

She disappeared back into the room where she'd made the coffee. At the edge of her buzzing, shrilling awareness, Sierra heard the liquid splosh into a sink, then the sound of another door opening and closing, and Cookie's feet on the wooden planking of the dock. She'd left via the back entrance, and Sierra and Ty were alone.

Alone.

For the first time since the take-it-or-leave-it, marriage-busting conversation that Sierra remembered every word of, even after eight years. Ty had left Landerville that same day, and he hadn't been back since. They hadn't even spoken on the phone.

They should have done.

They should never have let things drag out for this long.

"I guess I know why you're here," he said. He looked wary, and ready to be angry if the right trigger came.

Sierra's heart thudded suddenly. "Do you?"

"I wondered if you'd see the magazine."

"If I'd see it?" She laughed briefly. "Sometimes I feel as if everyone in America has seen it."

"You could have called." He mimicked a voice every bit as perky as Cookie's. *"I saw the cover story. Photos came out great. Congratulations."*

Perky, but with a metallic edge.

"You know that's not why I'm here." Her voice sounded scratchy, and not nearly as strong as she wanted it to.

"Wait a minute," he drawled, in mock surprise. "You're not here because of *A-list?*"

"Don't do this." Okay, that was better. Harder. "Yes, I'm here because of *A-list*. Of course I'm here because of *A-list*. But not to—"

The nautical bell jangled again at that moment as the front door opened, and Ty took a couple of backward steps into the doorway that led from the front office to the short corridor, then froze as if it might be dangerous for him to move in either direction.

A woman stepped awkwardly inside the building. She looked to be in her mid-thirties, and was dressed in a too-tight cutesy sailor suit with navy shorts, a striped top, and a red sailor-style neck tie, all of which the sales assistant in Silly Outfits 'R' Us really should have talked her out of.

"Um, I was wondering about sailing classes," she said, shyly ducking her head.

"Sure," Ty answered cheerfully. He wore the same smile showcased to such stunning effect on the front cover of *A-list,* but he still hadn't moved. To Sierra it looked as if he might make a run for it when he did. "We're pretty full, right now, but I'm taking down contact details, because we're putting together some extra classes."

"And will those extra classes be handled by… uh…by you personally. Um. Or will they be, um, taught by someone else?"

Ty's smile tightened a little. A stranger might not have spotted it but Sierra did and she was stunned at how well she remembered details about him like this. "Not sure, at this stage," he said.

"Because I'd rather be handled by you personally."

"I'm sure you would."

"Oh!" The woman suddenly clapped her hands to her mouth. She blushed and giggled. "I didn't mean that to come out the way it did! I'm so sorry!" As with the sailor suit, the blush, giggle and hands on mouth were not a good look for her. She took several steps closer and reached out, as if itching to give him an apologetic and lengthy squeeze. "I'm really so, so sorry!"

"We're actually closed right now," Ty said

quickly. "Could I ask you to come back at eight, when our office opens, and give your details to my assistant?"

"Oh, of course." She reversed direction like a mechanical toy, and the hands went back to the mouth, muffling another repetition of, "I'm so sorry."

She backed up to the door, dragged one hand from her mouth long enough to grab the doorhandle, edged through the narrow opening she'd made, and pulled the door shut with a slam. The nautical bell protested as if it, like Ty, had showcased its skills for too many similar women in recent days.

Ty sighed. "Can we close this place up and go grab coffee somewhere else?" he said to Sierra. "I appreciate that you want to talk."

His eyes flicked over her, taking in—probably—the way she'd aged, and the conservative outfit of matching skirt and top that she wore. They'd seemed appropriate, in her hotel room this morning, for an assertive confrontation with her husband. Now they made her feel plain and staid.

"Talking makes sense," Ty was saying. "We've both been stubborn about the situation for far too long. But it's obvious we'll never be able to do it here."

"No?" Sierra wasn't sure that she liked the idea of having this conversation in public, even if "public" did mean the quietest corner of that café she'd passed on her way here. On the other hand, a more private location had its downside, also.

"You think that sailor suit gal is the first?" Ty drawled. He leaned his elbow at head height against the doorjamb, as if he'd already reached the end of a long day.

"Uh, not from what your assistant said, no. But I'd have thought the extra traffic was good for business."

"Extra traffic? The whole of Garrett Marine has been under siege from the day *A-list* hit the stands." He glanced through the full-length front windows and along the boardwalk that led back to the waterfront's other businesses, spotted a pair of female figures moving toward the office and decreed, "Out the back way. Now. I'll lock."

This time, Sierra didn't argue. Didn't even say, "Serves you right," although she couldn't help thinking it.

And that really was mean-spirited.

Get a grip, Sierra. Cool down.

Ty locked the front door, dimmed the computer screen, switched off the interior lights and ducked into the back room, all in the space of seconds. Sierra followed him, hearing a disappointed, "Oh, they're not open yet," through the glass door behind her.

"Let's roll," Ty said.

He grabbed her arm and pulled her around the side of the small office building, so they could escape down the boardwalk while the two women were still reading Garrett Marine's office hours on the sign hanging against the glass. His palm and fingers felt warm against her skin, and his grip was as strong and confident as ever. Metaphorically, he'd tried to pull her from Landerville to Stoneport in exactly the same way.

Grab.

Roll.

Go where I want, never mind your own plans.

Back then, on that issue, she'd objected. This time, since it was just coffee and a long overdue conversation, she didn't. His hand on her arm felt better than she wanted it to, however, and the way he moved was like a charge of energy that overflowed into her own body and brought her back to life. They covered forty yards in what felt like five seconds, and her heart beat sped up.

"Here we go," Ty said, and pulled Sierra into *Tides,* the café she had noted earlier.

"Hey, Mr. Garrett," said another perky female.

He didn't flinch, so Sierra guessed the girl was an employee, not one of the besieging women he'd mentioned. This must be the café described in *A-list* as part of his extensive and still growing business empire.

"We'll take the corner table," he told the waitress. "And can you…like…move the potted plants, or something?"

"The model boat?"

"Perfect!"

"I'll get Evan to help." She called someone from the kitchen and the two of them shifted a glass case containing the fully-rigged model of an old clipper ship so that it did a good job of blocking the corner table from general view. Nobody seemed surprised that this strategy was necessary, which lent credibility to Ty's claim that Garrett Marine was "under siege."

Once seated, he didn't wait for a menu, but ordered a Danish and black coffee for himself— "Just keep it coming, Gina, okay?"—while Sierra asked for a muffin and a cappuccino. Both orders arrived promptly, which meant they didn't have to spend long pretending they had nothing important to talk about.

Gina left to serve some new arrivals, and Sierra seized her opportunity, because there had already been interruptions enough. "Please don't pretend that you don't know exactly why I'm here," she said.

"Tell me straight out, and neither of us should have to pretend anything."

"If you want a divorce, Ty, ask for a divorce. That's all you have to do. Don't advertise yourself in a national magazine as being gloriously available, and wait for me to draw the obvious conclusions, the way the entire town of Landerville has."

"You think this was about me wanting a *divorce?* You honestly think—"

"I've had hints and innuendoes and the same tired jokes over and over, total strangers coming up to me in the supermarket wanting to know the exact status of—well, our marriage, if there is one."

"Okay, for a start, your Dad's been mayor for about a hundred years; you know no-one in a town like Landerville is going to consider you a total stranger. Your life is town property, and so was mine, before I left."

Sierra ignored him and went on, "My sisters

are acting like someone died, and Dad was threatening at one stage to—" But Ty didn't need to know about her father's threats to his son-in-law's safety. "It's been…very embarrassing," she finished lamely, knowing she hadn't communicated a fraction of what she felt.

"Embarrassing?" Ty echoed, on an impatient laugh. "Yeah, tell me about it! That sailor suit lady a few minutes ago was more subtle than most. Trust me, Sierra, I'm winning in the embarrassment stakes, hands down!"

"In that case," she told him with a sharp edge, "it might have been a good idea if you'd thought the whole *A-list* thing through a teeny-weeny bit, before you agreed to it, huh?"

His blue eyes narrowed. "I never agreed to it, Sierra! Is that the kind of man you think I am? Interested in that kind of cheap publicity? Hell, interested in getting dates for myself that way? Listen! The Bachelor of the Year headline was the journalist's idea, not mine."

"You could have said no."

"I had no clue she was going to present the boat rescue story like that, until it appeared in the magazine. I didn't realize how much she was going to hook it into my business success, or that it would be on the cover. Let alone that it would bring this kind of response from total strangers. This mess has just erupted. You have no idea!"

"Gee, all that extra money coming in for extra sailing classes. All the extra business in your restaurants and waterfront stores. Yeah, most tourist enterprises really hate feel-good national publicity, I'm sure!"

He frowned. "Don't do that thing with your mouth. It doesn't suit you."

"What thing?"

"Looks like you're sucking on a lemon." Still frowning, he reached across the table and tried to do something to her lips with his fingers, the way he might have brushed a crumb from a child's cheek. What on earth…?

Smoothing them out? Yes, soothing those tight little muscles around her mouth.

With his touch, Sierra could feel the tight muscles herself, and wondered if that was why her face so often felt stiff and tired by the end of the day. Even before this whole mess with the magazine, she'd had so much on her plate.

There was her teaching job, working with a class of special needs kids, and three younger siblings who still depended on her a lot, and

Dad's health to monitor—he tended to leave the treatment of his diabetes largely to her—as well as his role as Landerville's mayor to support.

She knew she needed a vacation, but…sucking on a lemon?

Ty's finger-tips moved cool and light against her skin, like a caress, but still she flinched away and drawled, "Gee, thanks!"

"You're doing it again."

"Maybe because of all the extravagant compliments you're paying me."

"And again."

"Ty, do you or do you not want a divorce?" she blurted out desperately.

"You wouldn't contest it?"

Okay, Sierra. Don't sigh. Don't suck on a lemon.

She lifted her chin, managed not to gust out the big whoosh of air that tightened her chest, and said quietly, "No, of course I wouldn't contest it."

"You've had eight years to file for one, and you haven't."

"No, I haven't. Neither have you. But I want to, now. It's way overdue, don't you think?"

Of course she was right, Ty conceded to himself. About seven years and eight months overdue, probably. He should have filed the papers himself, as soon as he'd realized that she had called his colossal, confident, angry bluff and really wasn't going to follow him to Stoneport.

But he'd been stubborn about it. That was how he'd dealt with the hurt, by channelling it into sheer pig-headed pride. He wasn't the one making their marriage impossible. He wasn't wrong about any of this! Let Sierra take the steps to legally sever their union, if that was what she wanted.

She never had.

He'd been so cocky at twenty-four, so sure of himself, his goals, his decisions. "You know where to find me," he'd told her.

"And you know where to find me!"

And the hurt and disappointment had eased with time and hard work, the way such things did. The way they must have eased for her, too.

"If it's so overdue," he answered her at last, "why haven't you done something about it long before this? Why did it take some frothy magazine article to bring you here?"

She colored and shrugged, and paused for almost as long as Ty had, before she answered. "Let's just label it a wake-up call, shall we? Principles have a limited shelf life, I've discovered."

"Principles?" The word startled him. "Whose principles?"

"I'm not the one who walked out of our marriage. I'm not the one who wanted it to end. You did, Ty. So the divorce should have been up to you."

"I never walked out of our marriage! I walked out of Landerville."

"That's the same thing, isn't it?"

"No, it isn't! I was pretty clear on that at the time, I thought. There was no future for me there. Not one that could possibly have made me happy. I needed this." He swept his arm around, encompassing his world.

"What's 'this'?" She hooked her fingers around the word to make the quotation marks.

"The ocean, the boats, a chance to make a future for myself in a place where I wasn't just that more-or-less-orphaned Garrett boy who might get as far as managing the hardware store some day, if the love-struck mayor's daughter from the right side of the tracks could keep him honest. But you still don't get any of that, do you?"

"No, I don't. Dad never looked at you that way."

"The rest of Landerville did."

"You weren't just asking me to turn my back on a few narrow-minded attitudes. You were asking me to—" She stopped. Her cheeks were pink and angry and her dark eyes flashed. "A family is not something you can just walk away from, Ty. My family was not something I could just walk away from."

He sat up straighter. "I don't consider—I've never considered—that I was asking you to do that."

"Just listen to us!"

Sierra did the lemon thing with her mouth again and he couldn't find an answer. Yeah, listen to them! Back to square one. Back eight years to exactly what had slammed them apart in the first place.

She was so right. The divorce was overdue.

She sat there looking at him over the rim of her cappuccino cup and he took a moment to assess the changes in her. She'd been stunningly beautiful, to his eyes, when they'd gotten married twelve years ago. That graceful figure, as lean as a catwalk model's. That creamy skin. That wide, expressive mouth. That dark, straight, silky hair, flowing like a satin waterfall down her back. Those big, slightly exotic brown eyes—a throwback to some distant Cherokee heritage on her mother's side.

And she was still beautiful. The hair was the same, only kept a little shorter and folded into an efficient pleat high on the back of her head, this morning. The figure was a touch more womanly beneath its conservative olive and beige top and skirt, but if there was a man in this world who didn't like a few feminine curves in the right places, then that man wasn't him.

Her eyes and her mouth and her skin?

Yeah, beautiful.

Stunning.

Except…

She looked tired, at certain moments. Stressed. Angry? Unhappy?

And her eyes and mouth and skin were the places where the problems showed, whatever they were. The sucking on a lemon thing. A tightness to her skin which sketched out to the world where her wrinkles would some day appear. A way of narrowing those dark eyes so that the fire deep inside them almost looked as if it had gone out.

If the limbo of their non-marriage gave an explanation for any of this, all the more reason to get it dealt with so that both of them could get on with their lives.

Ty gulped some coffee and took a bite of the cherry and cream cheese Danish, wondering how best to get down to the nitty gritty of lawyers and such.

They had no kids, no joint property acquired during their four years together. And Sierra had never been the grasping type. On the contrary she was far too generous for her own good at times. She would never stake any kind of a claim on the wealth he'd acquired since their split, and even if she did no judge would award it to her.

He leaned closer to her across the table. "There's no reason why this can't be simple and amicable and quickly dealt with, right? Since it's what we both want?"

"No reason at all," she agreed.

"Then, yes, let's get it taken care of, get the ball rolling, before you head back."

"I'd appreciate that," she said. "No fuss."

"No going over old ground."

"No. Because we've—"

"Ty?" said a musical female voice that he recognized, and Sierra didn't get a chance to finish.

Ty looked away from her tight face to find *A-list* journalist Lucy Little smiling at him, much more casually dressed than Sierra in clam-diggers and a tight little black tank. She seemed as relaxed and at home as if she lived here, even though Ty had had no idea she'd planned to come back to Stoneport once she'd completed the magazine story that was causing all the current trouble.

He wasn't thrilled to see her, especially not at this moment. Sierra still looked so tight and emotional on the other side of the table, and his own feelings were attacking his sense of certainty like a guerilla-style ambush.

Before he could react to Lucy' greeting, she leaned down, cupped her hand around his jaw and kissed him European style, once on each cheek. The second kiss caught the corner of his mouth and trailed away slowly enough to signal unmistakable interest, and he remembered a couple of cryptic comments she'd made about professional boundaries and personal needs during the three days she'd spent here last month.

Okay…

He couldn't remember the exact wording, but the intent was much clearer, now. Their professional interaction was done with. Roll in the personal needs. Apparently all her questions about the state of his private life while she was researching the article hadn't simply related to the banner Bachelor of the Year headline he'd disliked so much.

"Lucy," he said, hiding what he felt behind the customary warmth he gave to clients. After all, the article had brought a serious surge in his cash flow. And it had brought Sierra, with her necessary wake-up call. "It's great to see you back in town."

"It's great to be here. You knew I would be, didn't you?" She looked at him through flirty lashes.

She pulled a chair across from the adjoining table and sat down, angling herself so that her veiled curiosity about Sierra wafted across one of her bare shoulders for a moment, disguised as a smile, then wafted away again. Sierra gave an uncertain smile in return, and took refuge in her muffin.

"I could have called, I know," Lucy said, her smile disarming and self-mocking now. "But I had to come find out in person whether you're pleased about the reaction to the article. We've had a ton of feedback at our end, let me tell you!" She gave a gurgly little laugh. "An astonishing number of e-mails and calls from women wanting your contact details. My editor is threatening me with a follow-up story."

"Threatening you?"

She pouted her mouth. "I'm technically on vacation time, this visit. Don't you remember what I said about professional boundaries, before?"

Yeah, he did.

Unfortunately.

The journalist wasn't his type. Nothing to do with her looks. Dark and willowy like Sierra, Lucy could have been her sister. But he'd never responded to the combination of little-girl giggles, seductive body language and man-eating aggression that she displayed.

He'd been as warm and courteous to her as their roles required, while she was working on the article, but apparently she'd read too much into that, and now he'd have to set her straight. At least the dozens of women who'd tried to flirt with him over the past couple of weeks had given him plenty of practice at getting his message across.

"What more could you possibly say in a follow up story?" he asked her, a little too blunt about it.

"Well, the reaction, of course. The women. *A-list* is primarily a celebrity gossip magazine, Ty, and you're a celebrity now."

Like hell he was!

"My fifteen minutes of fame?" he drawled.

"A lot longer than that, if you play it right." She sketched it all out, in far more detail than he wanted, while he gulped a refill of his coffee. Apparently, this could change his life.

No, thanks.

He liked his life just the way it was, apart from the small problem of needing an overdue divorce.

"Can I get back to you on that?" he said to Lucy, regretting again that he'd ever agreed to the original article.

He should have researched the magazine itself in more detail. He should have asked for the right to review and veto the article before it appeared. His main reason for agreeing to it had been to publicize issues about boating safety that he felt strongly about, particularly after the dramatic ocean rescue that could have cost four lives, and when he'd talked about all this to Lucy, she'd expressed only wide-eyed, enthusiastic agreement.

Boating safety? Of course! That couple should never have been out on the water by themselves in those conditions, for sure, and Ty was such a hero.

When the article had contained precisely one six-word quote from him on the risks he was concerned about, she'd apologized and talked about "my editor" and "cutting for length" and he'd taken her words at face value. Now, he wondered. He'd been uncharacteristically naive.

And he wondered, too, what would happen if he turned down a second article, point blank. Publicity and celebrity were two-edged swords. Never having experienced either on a major level, he'd over-looked this fact six weeks ago. But it didn't take much imagination or experience, now, to realize that one deliberately negative story could turn the tide of a successful business and threaten to destroy everything he'd achieved and worked for.

"I'm on vacation time," Lucy repeated. "Ten days. I told my editor I'd approach you regarding the second article, but nothing would be set in stone until my vacation's over. Even then, I might hand the story on to a colleague. Boundaries, remember?" Again, her eyes glinted at him through her lowered lashes. "My integrity as a journalist means I have to be objective, and…well…it's hard to be objective in certain positions…I mean situations."

Her giggly, suggestive tone reminded him of the recent and unfortunate sailor suit woman who wanted to be "handled personally." His heart sank.

Gina appeared again, leading two women to the adjacent table, from which Lucy had stolen her chair. She stood, apologized and slid it back. The two women sat down in a flurry of bag rummaging and menu shuffling and questions to each other about their sunglasses, all of which somehow managed to give them several long and unsubtle opportunities to look in Ty's direction.

Gina mouthed at him, "Sorry. Last table," and he realized that the place had filled up without him noticing.

There were a few regulars and a couple of tourist families, but most of the clientele was female, aged somewhere between twenty and forty, and every single one of them had either his Garrett Marine Sailing School brochure or his Stoneport Seafront Gallery brochure or his Nautilus Restaurant brochure in their hands.

He'd had each brochure printed with his own scrawled handwriting and signature. "Welcome to my world! Ty Garrett." An astonishing number of women had taken him at his word.

"I should catch you later when we'll have more time," Lucy said.

Deprived of her seat, she obviously felt that she lacked panache, standing there. People were craning past the fish tank to look at her. And at Sierra and Ty. And he was by this time a lot more familiar with this neck-prickling awareness of public attention than he'd ever wanted to be.

"Here's where I'm staying." Lucy flipped him

a card with the address and phone number of an upmarket bed-and-breakfast. "But I'll call you, so we can set something up." She gurgled her laugh once more. "Maybe I'll even take a private sailing class."

No.

This whole thing had to stop.

Now.

And he had to stop it at the source with something that neither Lucy nor anyone else in Stoneport could ignore.

Across the table, Sierra had quirked her mouth into a variation of the lemon thing that Ty couldn't interpret beyond a general sense that she wasn't impressed, and he realized that she represented the only obvious, tangible, workable solution to his current problem. If he didn't act at once, though, it would be too late. It wouldn't carry conviction.

He had to say it now, or not say it at all.

"Before you go, Lucy," he said, his voice as smooth and casual as he could make it. "I want you to meet Sierra, the most important woman in my life and, I should tell you, the reason you won't be able to call the next article Bachelor of the Year II."

"Oh, really?" Lucy cooed, with a dazzling, clueless smile. Clearly, she was still a couple of steps behind.

"Yes, really." He reached across the table and covered Sierra's smooth, pretty hand with his. He would have caressed her if he hadn't been so sure she'd snatch her hand away. "Because Sierra is my wife."

Chapter Two

"Just tell me, if it's not too much trouble, what that was for, Ty Garrett!" Sierra said to her soon-to-be ex-husband, through clenched teeth, as soon as the *A-list* journalist had gathered her shredded composure—her big-selling, drop-dead gorgeous Bachelor of the Year already, *excuse me*, had a *wife?*—and managed a more or less upright exit.

"Shh! Not yet," Ty answered. "Not here. Let's go."

He stood up and grabbed tighter onto the hand Sierra was trying to snatch away. Then he gave a quick tilt of his head to Gina to say they were leaving, and began to weave his way confidently

LILIAN DARCY

between the tables toward the café's kitchen door. At least a dozen pairs of female eyes tracked their progress, and as she followed him Sierra heard several whispered comments.

"That's him!"

"Lordy, what a body!"

"I have a private two-hour sail-boat cruise with him tomorrow…"

"Not here?" Sierra echoed, as the swing door closed behind them, shutting off the whisperings and the looks. The sounds and sights of a busy kitchen took their place. "Okay, Ty, we've tried your office, we've tried your café. What's next down the list?"

"Have to be my place, I guess," he said.

Well, I walked right into that one, didn't I?

She didn't know why it bothered her to think of continuing this confrontation with Ty on what was indisputably his own personal turf, but somehow it did. Maybe because she was too curious. She wanted to know what kind of a home he had set up for himself.

Sierra had gone back to live with Dad and her brother and sisters after the split and, because of their various needs, she was still there. In contrast, with no family ties and no budget constraints, Ty had only his own taste and lifestyle to consult. Did he inhabit a sterile bachelor pad? A designer decorated mansion? A permanent hotel suite?

She didn't want to feel so curious about him, when they'd just agreed on a divorce. Still less did she want to think that there might be any threat to her emotional health in being alone with him. She was over all that. She had to be, for her own well-being.

So why this sense of nerves jumping in her stomach, and pulses jumping everywhere else? Purely because this morning had been so much more complicated than she'd initially hoped?

The best solution would be to discuss everything they needed to discuss in private at Ty's, then get back to her motel, check out and leave town.

Still following in his wake, Sierra exited through the café's service doors and found herself in the access lane that backed the waterfront buildings. Since the lane largely serviced the various Garrett Marine businesses, she wasn't surprised to find it comparatively clean and well ordered.

The only item out of place was an ancient mud-brown sedan, parked crookedly so that it almost grazed the back wall of the next building and just left room for the delivery truck nosing its way past. The vehicle seemed to be one small step above a junk-heap shell, with dented panels, rusted bumpers and a silhouette that was thirty years out of style.

She nearly gasped out loud in disbelief when Ty aimed a key right for its passenger side lock.

"Decoy and get-away car," he explained, so apparently she actually had gasped out loud.

"This is—"

"The car I was driving when I left Ohio, yes."

"It looks—"

"Even worse. First three years here, it was the only car I could afford. I was plowing every cent that I could into the business, back then."

He opened the door for her and nudged her into the front seat with a gentlemanly gesture. She would have resisted, except that a glance at the interior told her it was neat and clean and—good grief!—uphol-stered with glove-soft taupe leather seats.

"Appearances can be deceiving, I guess," she drawled.

"Yeah, well, the original upholstery cracked and tore, and it seemed like I might as well replace it with something decent."

"I don't know why you kept this car at all."

Loyalty? Sentimentality? Was Ty like that?

"Told you, as a decoy," he said, as he arrived in the driver's seat. "Don't always want the whole town to know my movements. Which tend to be fairly obvious when I'm driving the Porsche."

"I wish you'd been as concerned for your privacy when *A-list* approached you about the article."

"Damn straight!" he drawled. "One issue we agree on, at least. Hindsight is a beautiful thing."

"So why that ridiculous announcement to the journalist, just now? If you want privacy in your personal life, why tell the world that you have a wife, especially when we're not going to be married a day longer than we have to be?"

"You saw what it was like, back there. And I'm sure your ears are as good as mine, so you heard, too. I've had it up to here, seriously, and notifying a very vocal journalist of the truthful fact that you and I are married seemed like a handy tool for dealing with it. You'll notice she didn't hang around."

"She's pretty."

"She's not my style. Neither was the sailor suit gal this morning. And none of the others were, either. And it's not how I'd choose to start a relationship, in any case, even if there had been a woman who'd made my heart stop beating and my breathing get stuck from the moment I first looked at her."

What would it be like, Sierra wondered, her own heart syncopating suddenly, to have Ty feel that way about her? Once upon a time he had. But he'd moved on since then, a lot farther than she had. His words hadn't been intended as a reminder, she knew. It was purely her problem that she'd taken them that way.

She said quickly, "The hordes might flood back again when they find out we're getting a divorce."

"Who's going to tell them?"

"People tend to notice when there's no visible evidence of a wife in a man's life, no?"

Ty swivelled in the driver's seat to face her. The car still sat crookedly in the lane, challenging the driving skills of another delivery man hard on the tail of the first, but he ignored the guy's problems and fixed her with a very serious, narrow-eyed gaze. It took him around four seconds to think the problem through.

"Then can I beg you on my bended knees to stick around for a bit, Sierra?" he said. "Help me out with this?"

"Stick around? *Help?* You mean act like we're still really married? Are you joking?"

"I don't think so."

"Work it out, and get back to me."

She put her hand on the door, intending to climb out, but he leaned across and stopped her, laying one arm across both of hers. She froze. His bare arm brushed her stomach, and would brush her breasts if she leaned just a little bit.

At one time they'd been way more intimate with each other than this, so she shouldn't feel uncomfortable about it. Problem was, his touch opened up too many memories, and too many lost possibilities.

"I'm not joking, okay?" he said, with his voice dropped low. "I want this whole situation to go away, and that pushy, man-eating journalist's attitude just now, on top of everything else, made me realize it's not going to, not on its own. Or not before it's driven me crazy, anyhow. I'm not the type to get my head down and wait out a storm."

"No…"

"I like to take action. I need to. You knew that about me eight years ago." True. "And it hasn't changed. So I'm asking for help."

"Now, *that* has changed," she couldn't help saying.

"What has?"

"You asking me for help."

"Yeah?"

"That's never happened before."

He shrugged, dismissing her claim as either untrue or unimportant, but she had a strong inkling in the back of her mind that he was wrong on both counts. "Well, it's happening now," he said. "Stay. Couple of weeks."

"I—I can't."

"You're on school summer break. Your family can manage without you. Some people consider Stoneport a great place for a vacation."

"I don't need a vacation."

He ignored the statement. "My place is big enough for us to keep out of each other's way," he said. "And I'll be in my office or on the water most days. The only thing I'll ask is for us to go out together a handful of times. In the Porsche, so that we're noticed. Make it real romantic, so that everyone gets the idea. When the heat fades, we can each see a lawyer, and you can head back to Ohio with a new tan and some friendly divorce papers in your suitcase."

It sounded easy, when he put it like that, yet Sierra still told him, "That's insane."

Probably because her inner reaction was

insane. Her heart shouldn't race like this. Her head shouldn't spin. And she should absolutely not consider for a second that he was offering her a second chance at their marriage, because he wasn't, and neither of them wanted one.

After eight years?

When even without the *A-list* article he probably had half a dozen beautiful, eligible, perfect women dangling after him at any given moment?

And, most important of all, when none of their reasons for splitting up in the first place had changed?

"It's not insane," he told her. "It's practical. There's no risk, is there, if we try this? After all, we're already married, and on the verge of a divorce that any sane person could have predicted before the ink on our marriage certificate was dry. Nothing worse we can do to each other than that!"

"That's what you think about marriage? About *our* marriage?"

If he hesitated, it was only for a fraction of a second. "Pretty much." His voice sounded like gravel rolling slowly in a cement mixer.

Sierra felt both hurt and angered that he would look at their four years as man and wife so cynically. No wonder he hadn't been in any hurry about a divorce, before this. He clearly had no intention of falling into the marriage trap again any time soon, so he didn't need the legal freedom. For different reasons, neither had she.

Beyond the hurt and anger, however, she was still thinking about the fact that he'd actually asked.

Asked her.

For a favor.

More than a favor. He'd said he needed her help. Self-sufficient Ty Garrett, who'd once had a chip on his shoulder the size of a tree trunk and wouldn't have admitted to needing *anything* in case somebody noticed, and who in fact never had needed anything, judging by the success he'd made of his life without anyone else's input… That same Ty Garrett had just looked her right in the eye and asked for her help.

Sierra didn't have time to explore the reason why, but it was the thing that tipped the balance for her, in the end—the fact that he'd actually asked for her help. If it wouldn't create problems for her family, she would stay in Stoneport a little longer and do what Ty wanted. Along the way, she might get a few answers to questions about their marriage that she hadn't known she still had.

"I'll have to call home," she said, and saw him frown.

"That's your basis for a decision? Whether you're needed at home?"

"It's a factor."

He was silent for a moment as if debating his reply, but finally he just shrugged and said, "We'll head out to my place, then. Take a look at it, see what you think, and you can make the call."

He took the back streets, leaving Sierra with the impression of a town that had found its feet as an attractive vacation spot and commercial hub for smaller surrounding communities.

She saw old Victorian houses spruced up as antique stores, restaurants, craft boutiques and bed-and-breakfast enterprises. On the far side of the harbor, which opened onto the sheltered waters of Carteret Sound, she saw a nineteenth century brick warehouse converted to upscale apartments, and on the way out of town there were signs indicating a theme park, hiking trails and golf.

Within a few minutes, they'd left Stoneport behind to thread their way along Onslow Banks, where the road offered stunning glimpses of green and white Atlantic breakers rolling onto the shore.

"You're not in town?" she asked.

"Not far out. Another couple of minutes… Here."

Wow.

Not a sterile apartment, not a lavish mansion, and definitely not a hotel suite. Instead, Ty had a year-round beach-house that was every bit a home. Set high up behind the dunes to put it out of reach of all but the strongest storms and tides, and surrounded by a wide wooden deck, it looked quirky and unique and as if it had grown in that spot.

It pretty much had, Sierra soon found.

"Built by one of the fishing fleet owners a hundred years ago," Ty told her. "When nothing else was out here. Quite an eccentric guy, I understand. It started out as just a cottage, but his descendants added to the place over the years which is why it looks…a mess, I guess."

"No!"

"You don't think so?"

"It has character." Sierra forgot to feel self-conscious about telling him what she really thought. "Feels as if it's inviting me in, to explore. That little window up top is winking at me, and that set of stairs disappearing round the corner is asking if I can guess what I'll find."

"Round the corner? There's a bench and seats built into the deck. Then there's a kind of Florida room, with a— You'll see. Come in and make that call to your family."

"They'll be fine, I'm sure," she said, then realized it sounded like a definite commitment to stay. "But if they're not, then the deal's off," she added, offering herself a way out.

He led her, business-like, into a large living area that opened onto a stunning deck, and pointed to a phone sitting on a small antique desk. "That's my private line. I have a business line in my office, right here, and I need to make a couple of calls myself, so just make yourself at home."

He indicated the direction of kitchen, bathroom and spare-room, then disappeared into the adjacent office, and Sierra sat down at the living room desk and picked up the phone. Her youngest sister Lena answered and assured her, "We're fine, Sierra. Absolutely. Don't worry."

"You're making sure Dad tests his blood sugar levels when he's supposed to, right?"

"He took a test yesterday—"

"Just one?"

"—and it was a little high. But don't worry. I'll nag him about it."

"And did Angie pick up the dry-cleaning? Because he has that big function on Saturday and he needs the suit."

"I'll check. But you'll be back by then, won't you?"

"I'm thinking of staying a little longer."

"Why? Ty's not making trouble, is he? Won't he give you the divorce? I'd have thought he'd be only too happy about it."

"Yes. No. I mean, yes, we're both only too happy about it, but that's not it."

How should she explain?

She sat back in the chair and let her gaze drift to the view from the windows on the far side of the room. Across the undulating, sea-grass-covered dunes, the Atlantic Ocean crashed onto the beach, perpetually scouring it clean. The summer air made a symphony of color and light—dazzling sun, powdery sky, salt spray hanging like a transparent curtain.

It was so beautiful that it hurt, and it did something to her soul that felt painful and good at the same time, like an aerobic stretch.

"He's…asked me for help with something, that's all," she continued to Lena. "And I kind of feel that I owe—"

Lena wasn't interested in what Sierra kind of felt she owed. "How long?"

"Ten days, maybe a couple of weeks."

"A couple of *weeks?* I have summer classes, and my job, and Dad's going to want one of us to do your First Lady thing at the dinner on Saturday, if you're not here. To be honest, Sierra, his blood sugar was, like, quite a lot too high yesterday. I didn't want to worry you…"

Sierra felt her temples tightening. She closed her eyes and forgot about the view of the ocean.

Okay, she'd have to coach Lena or Angie through the blood sugar and insulin thing again. Or Dad himself. But he just didn't seem able to grasp it, with all the other commitments he had between his business and his city hall duties, and anyhow he always thought she was over-reacting. So what if his sugar level was a little high?

"Well, okay, ten days," she said. "Max. I guess it shouldn't take more than that to…uh…handle this problem Ty needs help with. Maybe even just a week."

Maybe she could tell Ty he was on his own. He'd spent the past eight years proving that he could be happy that way. Why should his brief admission of need strike her as so important?

She took a big breath and said to Lena, "Listen, I'm going to print out an exact summary of what Dad needs to do, at what times of day, and what he needs to watch out for, and I'm going to fax it to you. I'm sorry, I thought he had a better handle on it after all this time. His doctor is a phone call away, and so am I, on my cell or here, and the bottom drawer of the desk in my room is filled with diabetic education brochures and booklets."

"Booklets?" Lena sounded skeptical and daunted.

"They're actually not that hard to read and understand. You and Angie and Jordy were too young when Mom died, so I took over from her with managing Dad's illness, but you're all old enough now."

Even during the years of her marriage, Sierra had stopped in at Dad's a couple of times, most days, to help him with his shots and his blood sugar tests. She'd also helped him as much as she could with the younger three, and handed out leaflets for his mayoral election campaign.

She finished, "I'm not expecting you to push Dad to handle it himself. I'll do that when I get back."

How? Dad was stubbornly determined to stay as ignorant as possible about his disease.

Sierra decided to ignore this problem until she was actually home again.

"You can handle it, okay?" she said to her twenty-two year old sister, using the same encouraging tone she used to her special needs pupils when they struggled with their math.

"Yeah, I know," Lena said. "But we just really miss you, okay?"

Which was why Sierra let herself remain the lynch-pin that kept the whole Taylor family together and functioning, ultimately. Because she knew she was loved.

"I miss you guys, too," she said, then gave Lena the phone number here at Ty's and ended the call.

Apparently Ty himself was still busy in his office, and the door was closed. He'd told her to make herself at home so she explored a little. Huge, gorgeous granite and wood kitchen; Florida room full of quirky, beachy furniture; wide wooden deck; powder room with decor befitting a five-star New York hotel.

Like the living room, the spare-room he'd designated for her overlooked the dunes and the ocean, on its own up a flight of stairs right at the top of the sprawling, higgledy-piggledy house. Since the room had windows on three sides, Sierra could see up the coast as far as the opening into Carteret Sound, and down the coast as far as a tall Carolina lighthouse with its broad, distinctive stripes.

French doors opened out to a narrow, wood-railed balcony that also skirted the room on three sides. A widow's walk? Was that what it should be called? Sierra wondered about it as she paced to one end of the balcony and back again, before pausing just to lean on the railing and look at the beach. She didn't know for sure. She'd only been to the Atlantic shore twice, both times down in Florida, which had felt very different to this.

Taking a deep breath of the fresh, salty air, she felt a surge of energy and anticipation that made sense when she thought about how long it was since she'd taken a real vacation.

Years.

Ever?

Never on her own, for sure. Dad wouldn't have felt safe about her doing that, in case his diabetes gave him trouble. She and Dad had always gone to places that were easy, like Disneyworld with Lena, Angie and Jordy when they were younger.

Once they'd taken a special cruise with medical facilities on board that were equipped to handle diabetic complications. That had been fun. And relaxing, when Lena and Angie weren't fighting. They'd been sixteen and seventeen then, which meant the cruise had happened, gosh, six years ago, already.

"I'm on vacation," Sierra said aloud.

The breeze caught her words and took them away out to sea, so she said it again, louder. "I'm—on—vacation!" And then she laughed.

It felt good.

But it got more complicated as soon as she heard Ty's voice, calling her from downstairs. The vacation came with conditions and obligations attached.

"I need to get back to the marina," he told her as soon as she came down to him. He already had car keys jingling in his hand. "How about I drop you at your hotel on the way? Then you can check out, and— You drove from Ohio, right, so you have your car?"

"Yes."

"Can you find your way back here? I'll give you a map for back-up. And a key, of course, and a garage door opener. The alarm's easy. I'll show you the code."

"I'll be fine."

"And your folks are okay?"

"Seem to be." She didn't mention Dad's blood sugar, or Lena's doubts about the proposed length of her absence. Maybe this really would only take a few days.

She noticed that Ty had never actually asked if she agreed to his plan. He just assumed she'd found the house and the sleeping arrangements satisfactory and her family's reassurances good enough. Typical, on his part. But she didn't feel inclined to protest about his assumptions now.

"So drop off your stuff here," he said. "Get settled in your room, have coffee, sunbake on the deck, whatever you want."

"Type up something on your computer and fax it to Ohio?"

"Sure. I'll leave you my cell number in case you have any trouble with the machine."

"Okay. Thanks."

"Then it would be…really useful…if you could meet me at the marina office, in a very public way, and we can go for lunch at the bar. That's pretty casual. Tonight, dinner at Nautilus would be great, and that's dressier, so if you didn't bring the right clothes I can give you the names of a couple of boutiques and you can shop for something this afternoon."

"Okay."

"I'll cover the tab, of course. Tomorrow—shades of irony, here—I'm dining with the mayor, who's a friend, and it'll be pretty formal, so if you could get a second dress—"

"How about you print out the full program for me with wardrobe requirements, as a handy reference," she cut in.

He stopped with his hand stretched to open the door leading to the double garage, and looked at her.

She glared at him. "Don't say that thing about sucking on a lemon again, okay?"

"Actually, I was going to apologize."

"For the lemon thing?"

"For bull-dozing you too much. Do you need more time? Are you committed to this?"

"Are you offering me an out?"

"We've both agreed on an out where it counts, with the marriage."

Not "our" marriage, she noticed. Just "the" marriage. As impersonal as you could get. Not

that she wanted to argue with that. But it was…
sad. Even after so long.

"I'm committed," she said.

Maybe if they could spend a few civilized,
conflict-free days together, she wouldn't go home
to Ohio with quite such a sense that they'd both
failed. Maybe she would discover why his admission of need seemed important.

"Great!" he answered. "We can make this work
exactly the way we need it to, I know it." Sierra
would have liked a couple of words added, like
"thanks" and "I really appreciate it," but she
wasn't surprised when they didn't happen.

In his garage, she discovered the silver
Porsche, holding pride of place right in the
middle, with plenty of space on all sides. The
poor, loyal old decoy sedan was relegated to a
stretch of raked gravel at the side of the house,
where anyone snooping around would see it and
think it belonged to the yard man or the cleaner.

They roared back into town in the Porsche, and
when Sierra went to the hotel's front desk to
check out after Ty had roared off again, the man
at the desk asked her at once, "You a friend of Mr.
Garrett's?"

"Sort of," she said. Not the answer Ty would

have wanted, so she added, "His wife, actually."
She saw the raised eyebrows across the desk, but
didn't deal with them because she was too busy
dealing with the strange feeling inside her.

Ty's wife.

She'd said those words so proudly and so
happily for four years, all through college. Then
she'd gotten her first teaching job and he'd left
town, and she'd never said them again.

Who knew it would churn her up so much,
saying them now?

Chapter Three

Ty's marina office was crowded when Sierra arrived back there and let herself quietly in the front door, at just on twelve-thirty. She'd changed into black stretch pants, open-toed shoes and a pretty pink top. She'd also let her hair fall loose down her back, painted her toenails to match the top, and put on dangly earrings and a gold bracelet, in the hope that she looked right for her new role as the wife of a wealthy man in a casual waterfront town.

She counted eight women milling around the space, after their morning sailing class. Six of them were young, skinny and gorgeous, while the other two would have passed for young, skinny and gorgeous in a softer light. There was also a single, solitary male, around twenty-five, who looked as if he couldn't believe he'd been so lucky today. Cookie stood behind the desk, dealing with questions and the phone.

"So fun!" said a tanned blonde.

"I'm going to take a week of full-day classes," replied someone else.

"Will that be with Ty?"

"That's a course pre-requisite, as far as I'm concerned. Where is he? Still, you know, folding sails or whatever?"

"I think so. I'm going to hang around." The blonde took out her cell-phone in order to camouflage her intention to stall. "Just for a bit. In case…"

The lone male asked one of the other women if she'd be interested in grabbing some lunch. She hesitated for a moment, as if weighing her chances at hooking a bigger fish, but then she smiled and said, "I'd like that," and they both looked pleased with themselves.

Maybe Ty's next business venture should be a waterfront dating agency.

Sierra cleared her throat and spoke over the noise of female voices. "Cookie?"

"Oh, hi, Sierra." With the phone to her ear, Cookie waved and smiled, as if she'd known Sierra for half her life. She'd obviously been briefed.

"Is my husband around, do you know? We're supposed to be going to lunch."

The door in the adjacent office opened at that moment, and Cookie called out, "Ty? Sierra's here for your lunch."

Jaws dropped.

Conversations dried up like shallow puddles in the sun.

Sierra felt a spurt of wicked pleasure that shamed her as soon as it happened.

Yes, that successful, gorgeous man is my husband, but don't go off to drown your sorrows, ladies, because this is all an act and we're getting divorced as soon as we can. Our marriage didn't make the grade. In truth, I have nothing to gloat about.

Thinking this, she suddenly wondered about the shape of her mouth. Lemons, again? She'd never thought of herself as a bitter person in any way, but maybe -

Ty appeared.

"Sierra!" His face lit up as if he'd arrived in port an hour ago after being ship-wrecked at sea for a month. It was an excellent performance. "I won't be back in today, Cookie," he said, and everyone in the room probably imagined, from that look still on his face, that he'd be spending the whole afternoon in bed.

With company.

They were wrong, of course. He had a bigger office, one block back from the waterfront, where several staff managed business activities more complex than booking boat charters and sailing classes. Cookie would find him there, once lunch was over, if she needed his input on anything. She knew it. Ty knew it. Sierra knew it. Everyone else was more than welcome to draw a different conclusion.

"Ready, sweetheart?" he cooed at Sierra.

The tanned blonde snapped her cell-phone shut and fronted up to Ty, not afraid to be direct. "So!" she said. "Bachelor of the Year?"

"Journalists don't always get the smaller details right, unfortunately," he answered, with a regretful grin, and dropped his arm around Sierra's shoulder. It felt way too nice in that position.

They strolled along the waterfront together in a silence that only pretended to be comfortable, until they reached the *Crow's Nest* bar.

As soon as they were seated, at the best and most visible table, facing the water, Sierra told him, "I'm not going to enjoy any of this."

"Never fancied yourself as an actress?"

"No, I haven't."

"You'll only be on stage a few hours a day. We just have to wait and see how quickly word gets out and the heat fades. We won't make it last longer than it has to."

"Yes. Good."

Like the café this morning and the Garrett Marine office just now, the bar was crowded. A few men. Lots of women. The men watched the women, and the women watched Ty—along with his mysterious companion, about whom rumors might already be flying.

Sierra took refuge in scanning the menu, and Ty said, "Yes, let's order, then get this show on the road."

She chose a chicken caesar salad and a white wine spritzer to drink, because plain water wouldn't look very romantic. As soon as the waiter had taken their menus, Ty reached across and took her hand, lacing his fingers through hers and leaning close.

"This is the show?" she murmured.

"Yep. Take your cue, Sierra. Lean in a little. Listen and talk as if this is the best conversation you've ever had."

"Oh! Easy!" she drawled.

It wasn't, actually. It was shockingly hard. The entwining contact of that strong brown forearm and hand with hers distracted her and turned her brain to instant mush. She couldn't think of a word to say, and remembered, suddenly, the very first real date she'd had with Ty when she was sixteen.

He'd taken her to the local outlet of a national restaurant chain that was just one step up from fast food take-out. Even that was probably way beyond his budget, at that time. And he'd had to do all the work—asking her questions, drawing her out.

In hindsight, he'd had a persistence and gener-osity that most eighteen year old men…boys… would never have managed in the face of her par-alyzed reaction. It had taken at least six dates before her wild feelings for him allowed her to relax enough for them to actually get to know each other. And then they'd talked non-stop about a hundred different things for hours and hours.

This memory didn't shed any insight on what was wrong with her today. She wasn't sixteen any more…

"Would have been easy, once, for us, a conversation like that," Ty said, after he'd watched Sierra's thoughtful face for a long moment. He heard the husky note in his own voice with a degree of shock. "Easiest thing in the world."

Hell, where had that come from, he wondered? Not just the intimate tone, but the words themselves. Why on earth would he want to create any sense of nostalgia about this? He and Sierra were finished. Done. Over it.

You couldn't go back. Not when none of the problems had gone away.

"So tell me about your work," he prompted, aware of their silence and the conviction that was sadly lacking in their performance. He softened his grip on her hand, making it into more of a caress, and he didn't take his eyes from her face. "You got into teaching special needs kids, the way you wanted?"

"Yes, I did and I love it."

"Can't always be easy."

"I had a tough class this past year," she said, nodding. "A couple of kids who needed a lot of time and attention, with difficult family backgrounds to deal with, also. On top of that, I'd put together a science program for my kids a couple of years ago, and I was asked to adapt it for use in other schools."

"That's great, Sierra!" Typical of her that she should play it down.

"It was," she answered. "My school principal kept telling me how good it would look on my résumé."

"Your principal was right."

"At the same time, though, it kept me busier than I needed to be!"

"And your family? How are they doing? They must all be grown up now."

Ty hadn't heard Sierra's phone conversation this morning, but remembered that it was the first thing she'd talked about in relation to staying here longer. "I'll have to call home," she said.

To see if the rest of the family could survive without her. This had been the clear implication.

Sierra's sisters had been fourteen and fifteen when he'd left Ohio eight years ago, and her brother Jordy had been eighteen. By now, they should be in college or out in the world with jobs and responsibilities. Spouses and babies, even. They shouldn't depend on her so much.

As for her Dad…

If he hadn't changed drastically over the past

eight years then he was still a good man, hard-working and committed to serving his local community. But he'd always used his heavy schedule as a shameless excuse to abdicate all responsibility regarding his own health. Not quite a part of the family, Ty had seen it years ago and had suggested to Sierra a couple of times that it wasn't a good thing, not for Mayor Taylor or for Sierra herself, but she hadn't really listened.

"I lost Mom when I was fourteen," she'd told him then. "I'm not going to lose Dad. If I have to nag him, and keep track for him, and take him for his check-ups, then I'll do it. He has too much other stuff to deal with. He's not going to take it seriously on his own."

"Maybe if he had to, or if he had a scare," Ty had suggested.

"A scare?"

"A stint in the hospital, or something."

She'd looked horrified at the idea, and in hindsight, he couldn't blame her. Not everyone reacted to challenges the way he did, wanting to take action, fight, learn, change.

"The family is all grown up," she agreed now. "Jordy's selling real estate, which he's very good at, and loves. He's still living at home but looking for his own place. He might move to Cincinnati. Angie's just finished her senior year of college at Ohio U. in Athens."

"Pre-law, I'm guessing."

Sierra smiled, looking happier than he'd seen her all morning. Her sudden pleasure lit up her whole face and she looked a good five years younger, especially with her hair flowing loose down her back and those funky little earrings. She was proud of her sister. "How did you know?" she asked.

"She was always a bright little thing," Ty answered. "And she never missed an episode of any TV drama that dealt with the law."

"She's hoping to start her law degree at Ohio State in the fall, but she may move up there sooner than that. Her boyfriend Todd has been in Columbus since the start of the year, working for a big corporation, so she can't wait and she's getting antsy."

"And Lena?"

"Starting senior year, also in Athens. But she wants to teach like me."

"You should be very proud, Sierra, because so much of it is down to you. You've been practically a parent to them from when you were only a kid yourself."

"Well, you know, I've tried. It's what you do, in my situation. When you lose your Mom."

He leaned closer, watching how self-conscious she'd become, how she colored and again tried to play down her own input. In his soft grip, her fingers worked back and forth, long and lean and cool. "No," he told her. "Not everyone sees it that way."

"Well…" She smiled. And sighed. And looked over her shoulder with an expression of relief. "Here comes our lunch!"

"So we can let go of each other, you mean?" He dropped his voice and deliberately watched her mouth. "Was it that bad? Touching each other?"

Hell, Garrett! Again! First nostalgia, and now flirting. Neither of those things were on their agenda. His only excuse was that both would enhance their performance as a blissfully married couple.

Sierra didn't answer his last question directly, just picked up a chicken wing and began to eat. After a few moments she said, "Let's get our story squared up on this fictionally successful marriage of ours. Is it supposed to be a recent thing, or are we sticking to the facts?"

"We can let people think what they want, can't we? As long as they think we're happy together, it doesn't matter if we're newly-weds or old-timers in their eyes."

"We might get questions. I think we should get our story straight."

"Okay, then let's stick to the facts. We've been married twelve years."

"So where have I been all this time? Not in Stoneport, clearly."

"We've had a long-distance marriage. We commute because of conflicting commitments in different places. It works for some people."

She made a face and Ty thought, yes, I'd hate that, too.

He didn't tend to do things by halves. When he wanted something, he worked for it. When he felt something, he felt it through and through. Joining his life to Sierra's twelve years ago had encompassed every facet of his being—body, mind, heart and soul.

Apparently she felt the same about what marriage meant. Maybe that was why a compromise had been so unthinkable for both of them. They needed either joined lives, or separation without so much as a phone call. Something they had in common. They were the all-or-nothing type.

And they'd ended up with nothing.

"That's the most plausible story, I guess," she said.

"And only if we're asked. I have stuff I have to get done this afternoon, Sierra. You do need to buy a couple of outfits for dinner tonight and tomorrow, right?"

"Well, I expect Stoneport will get pretty tired of the limited wardrobe I've brought, and most of it is too casual, anyhow. So, yes."

"After that, I could put you on a boat cruise if you want."

"Would that look right for Ty Garrett's wife? Playing tourist?"

"No need for you to be bored."

"I won't be. I'll go back to your place, lie on that deck in the sun, walk on the beach for a while."

Just saying it and thinking about it flooded Sierra with a sense of relaxation she hadn't experienced in a long time. Solitude. The sound of the sea. Sand under her bare feet, and the sun on her back. No demands on her energy or her time. No responsibility.

Mmm.

Unconsciously she closed her eyes in delicious anticipation, then felt Ty's finger brush her mouth, the way it had this morning in the café. Her eyes flashed open again and the mood was broken. "If you mention the word lemon…!" she said, while tendrils of awareness and need grew rampant in her body like tropical vines.

His blue eyes widened. "Hey, no. I was thinking the opposite. How soft your mouth looked." His gaze dropped to it, and she had a stab of powerful memory about the way they'd once kissed. It coiled all the way through her body like a hot wire, melting her. "Wondering just how much you need this break," he finished, in a different tone.

There was a criticism implied in his words, she just knew it. That coil of heat ebbed away. "I'm fine," she said. "I don't have to need it to enjoy it, do I?"

He shrugged, and in the silence that followed they both realized that people at several tables were staring at them. When he reached across the remnants of their meal and tenderly brushed a non-existent strand of hair back from her forehead, she knew it was only a part of their performance.

Ty got home at six that evening to glimpse Sierra stretched out face-down on a big colorful beach towel on his ocean-facing deck in a patch of warm sun. From this side of the house she obviously hadn't heard the car, the garage door, or his footsteps across the floor, because she hadn't stirred. Might even be asleep.

He hadn't had much time to think about her this afternoon, plunged into the familiar juggling routine that was required to keep all his different enterprises on track. He had talked to the owners of the clothing boutiques he'd recommended to Sierra, however, arranging credit for anything she might purchase, and now he felt a stirring of very male curiosity about how she would look tonight.

The curiosity shifted and took a more immediate form. Through the windows of his living room he could glimpse a lot of skin out there on the deck. A lot of skin, glistening with lotion, and not much fabric. Had she taken off…?

Yep.

No top.

And not much bottom.

He was just about to turn away, questioning his right to such a private sight when he and Sierra were only still married on paper, but then her cell phone trilled a nagging melody. She scrambled to sit up, looking sleepy and disoriented as she grabbed for her sun-glasses and the phone, and his view got even better. Quite fabulous, in fact.

No, Ty.

Reluctantly he turned away, hearing her voice. "Hi, Angie…again. What's up, now?" She listened for a moment. "Oh, he didn't?" Listened again. "No, it's easy. I promise. You just…"

At this point, Ty had walked out of earshot, but the whole scene stayed in his mind more vividly than it should have done. Sierra's straight back. Sierra's softly contoured front. Sierra's legs, long and graceful as she sat up, and the ultra-feminine bounce of her breasts. Sierra's voice, a mix of impatience and warmth and concern as she spoke to her sister, clearly not for the first time this afternoon.

He wondered if she'd gotten the relaxing hours she so clearly craved. He wondered if her family ever left her alone, or considered her needs.

A few minutes later, from his bedroom along the corridor, he heard her footsteps in the living room and called out a greeting to warn her of his presence just in case she hadn't gotten her swimsuit top back on yet.

She had, he discovered a minute later, when he entered the room. The view was still pretty spectacular, however, and he was way too conscious of the fact. The neat tuck of her long waist only emphasized the generous swell of her breasts above it, and her bright, tropical colored two-piece swim suit was cut as if Lycra was rationed this season, due to a shortage of supply.

How could he have forgotten the impact she'd always had on him? How could it have remained so strong after so long? He would ache all over again when she went back to that family of hers, the way he'd ached month after month when she hadn't followed him here eight years ago.

He didn't want to think about it. Definitely didn't want to let it show.

"I thought we could show up for dinner at around seven," he said, making his voice as bland as possible. "As long as that works for you."

"That's fine," she answered "I'll take a shower right now."

Not quite right now. Her cell-phone trilled again.

"You should really program in a different ring tone," he told her. "That one's unbearable."

She ignored him. "Hi… Dad, hi… Yes, Angie told me. You really, really have to remember to ask for Diet, okay? So how is it now?" She listened, then nodded. "That's not so bad. Could have been a lot worse."

"I'm taking a walk," Ty mouthed at her.

He could easily have chosen a cold shower.

By the time he'd gotten back to the house and dressed for dinner in a dark suit with a silvery gray shirt and tie, she was ready, and she took his breath away as she came down the stairs.

The brand new dark red dress made a wide V from the tanned knobs of her shoulders down to the first hint of shadow between her breasts. Lower down it clung to her figure as smoothly as a second skin before finishing just above her knees. High red heels made her legs look even longer and leaner, and she'd piled her hair up on her head so that her neck was bare and brushed only by dangling droplets of gold at her ears.

Her eyes looked darker than usual and her mouth looked fuller and more openly sensual, as if she'd sensed the effect she would have on him almost before she came into view, as if she wanted it and answered it with a reaction that was every bit as strong.

Don't let her see, Ty. Play it down.

Because where could this possibly go?

Nowhere.

The same old ground.

Desire was one thing. A marriage was different.

"You look good." He kicked the statement at her sideways as they walked through to the garage. It sounded like a polite formula he could barely trouble himself to get out.

"So do you," she answered, her voice a little thin. "I've never seen you in a suit before, but it looks, um, authoritative."

"In that case, we should make a convincing couple."

"Is this really achieving anything, Ty? How long before we can conclude that it's working, or it isn't? I'm not staying on here for days and days if there's no point."

"Is your family giving you trouble?"

"No. They're fine. Dad had a slight hiccup with his blood sugar because he forgot to check—" She stopped, then added, "It's not important."

Ty got the impression she might have been reminding herself of this, rather than informing him.

Nautilus had several groups of people crowding its elegant bar while waiting for a table, but the best one in the whole place was laid with a pristine cloth and silverware, in readiness for the owner and his beautiful wife.

Each knowing that they were the focus of attention at more than one table, they sat down, studied their menus, conversed superficially about the weather and the way the light kept changing across the harbor as the sun sank in the sky.

The photographer from the Stoneport Weekly came in as he often did on a Tuesday or Wednesday night, in search of a picture or two for the social pages since the newspaper came out on Fridays. Usually Ty gave him the thumbs down, but tonight he summoned man and camera and posed with his arm around Sierra's shoulder and a big, lucky husband type grin on his face.

"Get the caption right, won't you, Matt?" he said. "Ty and Sierra Garrett, at Garrett Marine's flagship restaurant, *Nautilus*. Something like that."

Sierra frowned at him as soon as Matt had cruised to the next likely-looking table. "I've never gone by Garrett," she said. "Remember? When we got married, I was already enrolled in college as Taylor, and on all the invitation lists with Dad as Taylor, and I just didn't get around to—"

"It's just a newspaper caption, Sierra," he told her with exaggerated patience. "It's not a legally binding document."

"Okay. You're right, I guess," she agreed, after a moment.

Sierra didn't know why it bothered her to suddenly hear herself endowed with a new name. Ty's name. They'd only embarked on this whole thing less than twelve hours ago, and they had solid motivations for it. There was no reason to fear it could get out of control.

Get out of control, how?

Only one way for it to do that.

If she was foolish enough to start wanting this. Wanting him. Wanting their marriage.

And she wouldn't, would she?

The meal was fabulous. They chose seafood to share—a sampler platter of oysters prepared half a dozen different ways, followed by lobster with mesclun green salad on the side. Ty chose the wine. He'd known nothing about the subject eight years ago but tonight he ran his finger down the extensive list like an expert.

He had the aura of a gourmet, too, in his expensive dark suit and well-schooled table manners. He hadn't been brought up to this lifestyle. As with everything else he'd achieved, he'd done it all on his own.

The sommelier deferred immediately to his

choice of wine. "You were right on the money, when you ordered that for our cellar, Mr. Garrett. It's a great vintage."

For dessert, Sierra couldn't go past chocolate—a rich mousse cake, with raspberry syrup making lacy patterns all around the edge of the plate—and since at a place like *Nautilus* you couldn't help lingering over a meal, it was almost ten by the time they'd finished their coffee.

"Want to take a walk around the marina?" Ty suggested. "The whole waterfront is busy tonight. Plenty of people to see us and feed the rumors."

"I guess I could stand a little more of this," she answered.

It sounded sour, she knew, but did he really have to remind her with every comment about why they were pretending this way?

The meal had been so perfect. Even their conversation had dropped to a more meaningful level pretty fast after the brief skirmish over her last name. She'd asked him about his boat charters and he'd told her how he'd skippered his biggest and most luxurious sailboat, *Moderation,* as far as Bermuda and Nantucket on different occasions for various well-to-do clients.

The animation in his face told her how much

he loved the variety and spice of adventure in what he did, and she felt as if they'd connected on a level she hadn't experienced for so long.

Now, with a couple of phrases, he'd reduced all that to a staged event.

Which it was.

So he was right.

Remember that, Sierra.

Outside, he put his arm around her, but they didn't talk and she had time to notice a couple of curious looks from passers by, as well as a little whispering that she couldn't catch. Conflicting stories must be circulating the town.

Was this really a long-distance marriage that Ty had never had occasion to mention before? Was it a reconciliation? Or were they newly-weds? Whatever the truth, it had to be clear to most people that the Bachelor of the Year thing had been blown out of the water.

"Good spot, do you think?" Ty murmured, when they reached the end of the long wooden dock where his charter boats were moored. The golden light from the windows of *Nautilus* stretched across the dark water, and ropes chinked against the aluminum masts in the mild evening breeze.

"Yes. Gorgeous spot," she answered, but that wasn't what he meant, it turned out.

"For me to kiss you."

"Oh. No. Ty. Do you think—?"

"Yes, I do think. It's essential."

He swung her lightly across the front of his body and tightened his arms around her, then looked down into her face. His mouth was only a few inches from hers and she could feel the whole hard male length of him beneath the fine woven wool of his hand-tailored suit. Thighs, stomach, chest.

He smelled of soap and coffee and fresh sea air, and it was lucky he was so strong, because she wasn't strong at all, right now. Her legs would buckle beneath her, if he let her go.

"A quick one, okay?" he said. They were pressed so close that she could even feel the low vibration of his voice against her body. "But soft."

Very soft, and not so quick. His mouth touched hers almost before he finished speaking, and it didn't go away. He tasted familiar, and yet as new as a foreign land. His lips were parted slightly, and they moved as if on a quest of discovery. Her own lips softened on a sigh of breath, and her eyes closed without her permission.

Crazy.

Dangerous.

She felt his finger brush the dangling length of her earring, so that it swung and tickled her neck. He slid his hand up into her piled hair, and some of the pins came loose. It would tumble down if he didn't stop, so she pulled on his arm to make him let go, then felt the heat of his touch all the way down her back.

"That's enough," she managed to say, even though she hadn't really stopped.

"No, it's not," he muttered. "It's nowhere near enough." And he tightened his arms around her, bent his head again, and sent her whirling into a place that for much of her adult life she'd forgotten could even exist.

Chapter Four

With the first touch of her lips on his, Sierra had turned Ty's universe inside out. That was how it felt. He couldn't think of anything except her body in his arms and her taste in his mouth. He couldn't remember what this was supposed to be about, or why it would have to end.

His whole body throbbed and he wanted her a dozen different ways. He wanted to make love to her with breathless impatience and with slow, teasing heat. He wanted her helpless with laughter in his arms, and sobbing with release. He wanted to shudder against her, enveloped in the fragrance of her hair and her skin, and then fall asleep in her arms and dream of heaven.

And, to be honest, hadn't he known it would be like this? Hadn't he ached for memory to become fresh experience all evening? Watching her expressive mouth while she talked, he'd hardly been able to tear his gaze away.

The memories were so vivid, too. All the trembling and the laughter and the tears that had happened the first few times they'd made love more than twelve years ago...

It all came back to him in such detail that he wondered how many times he'd dreamed about Sierra over the past eight years without even realizing it. Had he relived the sensual fulfilment of their marriage in the dark safety of his subconscious and then suppressed the dreams before morning?

When she told him, "That's enough," he'd barely started and he was sure she didn't want to end their kiss any more than he did.

Mmm, he was right.

She sighed against him, wrapped her arms tighter, let her body soften so that it fit the shape of his as closely as the sensuous fabric of her dress fit over her breasts. Her body had always been so responsive and he'd loved that—loved his own power to do this to her, loved her sensitivity and heat. He couldn't believe that none of it had gone away.

Sierra shifted her weight, trying to nestle herself even closer, and he felt the sharp heel of her shoe brush across his ankle, soft enough to feel like a caress. He kissed her neck and that dangly gold earring tickled his cheek. He closed his lips over it, and over her delicate ear lobe, let his breath blow hot on her skin and felt her answering shiver.

The ridge of his rapidly swelling arousal pressed into the soft, silk-sheathed warmth of her body and made him burn. If they'd been anywhere more private than this, he would have slid her dress down into a scarlet heap at her feet like a discarded flower. As delicious as that silky fabric was, he wanted her skin.

"That's enough, Ty…" she tried again, after another breathless interval.

Her hands were clamped to his upper thighs and her hips were locked against his. Her breathing pushed in and out with a ragged rhythm, and his name was just a part of their kiss.

"No," he told her. He slid his hands up her back and neck and into her hair, which fell over his knuckles and down her spine, flooding him with the sweet, flowery scent of her shampoo. She gasped. "I can feel how much you want this, Sierra, so why stop?"

"Because any second now, someone's going to tell us to get a room."

She didn't pull away from him, just closed her eyes tighter and tried to press her lips together, denying him entry. It didn't faze him. Her jaw and her neck tasted just as good as her mouth—like jasmine tea—and from her shiver of response they were every bit as sensitive.

"You have a point…" he told her. "And I have lots of rooms."

He wished they were in one of them now. Bedroom, living room, study, didn't matter. He'd take the broom closet if he had to.

This time she did pull back, giving a helpless whimper like a trapped animal. Her darkly dilated eyes begged him for a little assistance, even when her body begged him for something much more physical. Her breasts weren't molded to his chest any more, but he was still holding her close enough to feel the whip-tight tension that vibrated all through her.

"No. Please. Come on." She spoke softly although their only audience—it wasn't an audience; this wasn't a performance any more—was at least twenty yards away on an adjacent dock. "You know why we're doing this, Ty, and it's not as an appetizer before the main course. It stops here."

"Why?"

"Because we're getting a divorce. Because we're only doing this to hose down the heat from the *A-list* story. Do I have to *remind* you of that? Do I have to spell out to you that, no, I'm not the kind of woman who can casually jump into bed with my almost ex-husband for old time's sake? Nice farewell performance, Ty, thanks for the memories. No. I'm not that woman."

"That's not what I was thinking."

"Were you thinking at all? Everything that split us apart eight years ago is still there. Why make this any rougher on ourselves?"

"Are you saying it's already rough?"

For a moment she didn't answer, and when she did her voice had dropped even lower.

"Yes. It's rough. It's hard. I'm shocked and astonished and mystified that it's so hard. And that it was hard from the moment I saw you today, in your office." She shivered more violently in his arms and her muscles tightened. "And I'm wondering why I ever agreed to stay. My self-protective instincts weren't exactly working over-time this morning."

She stared down so that all he could see of her eyes were the black lashes feathered against her cheeks and her thick, creamy lids. But, hell, he knew her so well he didn't need to see her eyes to know what was happening inside her.

"Do you have any of those, Sierra?" he said softly. He lowered his face to brush his forehead softly against hers. "Self-protective instincts, I mean."

She reared her head back from the contact with a jerk. "Of course I do. What are you saying, Ty?"

"You give too much. You always have. You're doing it now. Giving so much, with one kiss. More than some women can give with their whole bodies and their whole souls."

Her mouth still looked swollen, moist and soft, as if she'd been eating chocolate and whipped cream.

"And you're just standing there and taking it?" she said. "Even while you're telling me it's not good for me?"

"Yeah, I think so."

His mind felt thick and slow right now and he

wasn't used to that, when usually he jumped from A to B so fast. Joining the dots. Making connections. *Understanding*. He didn't think he understood very much tonight, at all.

"I seem to be, don't I?" he went on, still vague. "Taking it and wanting more. Wanting so much more."

"Well, that makes sense! Thanks for your generous insights!" She twisted out of his arms, spun around and walked away, her shoulders hunched and tight with anger.

"Wait, Sierra!"

He caught up to her in seconds and curved his hands over those tensed, squared shapes, but she shook him off and didn't stop, her long legs beating out a rapid rhythm so that the two of them went stride for stride all the way along the dock.

His Porsche waited for them in its executive parking space beside the Garrett Marine office, its leather seats matching her hair, as if Ty himself believed that wives and cars should coordinate like the perfect shirt and tie. No wonder they were still getting curious glances and snatches of whispered commentary leaking from behind strangers' hands, with every knot of people they passed.

"Take me home," Sierra said, hand on the

Porsche's sleek door handle. Her dark eyes glittered and her cheeks were flushed.

"Yes, and then we'll talk." The car gave an electronic yelp as he pressed the code on his key fob.

She shook her head. "There's nothing to say."

"There is, if you're angry."

"I've been angry for eight years, Ty."

"So have I." He reached out and touched her hair, aching to feel its silky slipperiness through his fingers again. "Don't you think it's worth working out if one or both of us is right to be angry after so long, and how it is that we can manage to kiss hot enough to blister paint when we're about to file for divorce?"

"I—I don't want to examine any of that. I don't see how it would help." She yanked open the door and slid into the car, her body moving like a willow branch in the wind.

Before he could close the door for her, she grabbed it and did it herself. Slamming an expensive piece of precision engineering like a Porsche passenger door wasn't easy, but Sierra communicated the intent to slam loud and clear. By the time Ty was seated behind the wheel she had her own question ready for him, although she hadn't ever answered his.

"You're not saying—you *can't* be saying—that you want to reconsider the divorce?"

Yeah, and it was a good question, too.

Ty thought about it. Turned to her before she spoke. She looked scared, overwhelmed, hostile.

"No, I'm not saying that," he said slowly. "But doesn't this give us the chance to find some answers? Everything was so unfinished, eight years ago. It all hung there, locked in our stubbornness and our refusal to communicate after I left. This time, I don't want loose ends. I don't want anything holding me back. I want to move on."

"So do I. *So do I!* Shoot, Ty! Sleeping together wouldn't be the way to do it. That wouldn't tie up anything."

"No." Every cell in his body told him it didn't matter if sleeping together created more loose ends than a ripped sail. It would feel like heaven and he wanted it.

No questions asked.

No second guessing.

No regrets.

"We got married too young, that was all." Sierra's statement brought him back to earth with a jerk. "We got ourselves into a situation that didn't work for us in the long term. We're old enough now to get out of it without hurting each other or making any more mistakes, surely."

"Yeah, you'd think so, wouldn't you?" he drawled. With his thought processes still handicapped by the throb of need that radiated out from a place agonizingly constricted by his formal clothing, he couldn't keep the skeptical edge from his voice.

"We have control over this," she insisted. "We were too young, but we're adults now."

Adulthood, of course, and adult needs, could be a double-edged sword, and painfully sharp.

Biting hard on his lower lip he started the engine.

The door of Ty's garage rose noiselessly, echoing the silence that had filled the car for most of their journey home. All the way Sierra had wanted more from Ty, but in all honesty she couldn't have been specific as to what so it was hardly his fault that he hadn't spoken.

The beauty of the coastal night stirred her even more here in the dunes than it had at the Stoneport Marina. When the garage door slid down again, leaving them in darkness and air that smelled of car fumes, she felt claustrophobic and

anxious to escape upstairs, back to the deck she'd
enjoyed so much this afternoon, back to the sound
and smell of the sea, away from her awareness of
Ty and everything he'd done to awaken her
sleeping senses.

He let her go ahead of him, switched on a
couple of lights, then followed. Her neck tingled
when she felt the draught of air that his movement
made as they went up the stairs. If he came up
close behind and touched her, held her, put his
lips in place of the air kissing her skin, she
doubted she'd be able to push him away.

No, she would do the exact opposite. She'd
turn into his arms, bend her body close to his and
go hungrily in search of his mouth.

"I don't think we were too young, Sierra," he
said, just as they reached the living room.

He flung his jacket over the back of a couch,
took off his tie and rolled his shirtsleeves up as if
the atmosphere in here was too hot. Her own
flaming skin didn't suggest a contradiction.

"You were twenty," she answered defensively.
She still felt so jumpy at the minimal distance
between them. "And I was eighteen. That's
young. When I look at Lena and Angie and even
Jordy, it's so young!"

"Age isn't just about how many birthdays you've had," Ty answered.

"Isn't it?"

One side of his shirt collar had flipped up when he'd removed his tie and it nudged at his cheek, bright against half a day's growth of new beard. He pushed his hands deep into his pockets, adding to the brooding look of dangerous impatience that had invaded him.

"We both had to grow up fast, Sierra, don't forget. You, from the time your mom got sick. Me, from... Yeah."

From day one.

This was a sure-fire way to drain the heat from the atmosphere—Ty's childhood.

Sierra knew how much he hated to talk about it. When they'd first started going out, even though they'd been at the height of that teen stage where most kids are starry-eyed and trusting enough with each other to pour out their whole souls, she'd had to piece his story together like a quilt made from fabric scraps.

He'd never known his father, and his mother hadn't been around very much. She called herself a singer, and periodically she would disappear to New York or Nashville or the West

Coast for long stretches of time in search of fame and success, leaving Ty to be raised by his grandparents.

Sierra didn't know the exact details of the setbacks and side-tracks that Faith Garrett dragged into the picture to account for each successive failure, and if Ty knew more than he told she didn't want to push him on it. At minimum she suspected strings of bad lovers, incurable naivety, and a voice that might once have been pretty and strong but had been ruined by cigarettes and cheap living.

Meanwhile Ty's grandparents meant well, but they had their own problems, and how to spend an abundance of money wasn't one of them. They lived on a tiny piece of land where his vague, impractical grandmother ran a few chickens and his crafty, miserly grandfather fixed engines, and not everyone in Landerville considered that Burl Garrett's cheap rates were matched by honest service.

They were never in great health, and they'd always been dirt poor. Ty had been the most able-bodied and responsible member of the Garrett family since the age of six, and the only one left by the time he was seventeen.

So maybe he was right. Maturity didn't depend

on how many birthdays they'd each had. A lack of maturity hadn't been their problem.

"So what are you saying, Ty?" She watched as he pivoted around, dragged his hands from his pockets and opened the door that led to the deck. The night air flooded in, surfing on the sound of the waves, and they both followed its call.

Ty leaned on the wooden deck rail, his expression lost in shadow although the light that spilled from the house sheened the fine woven shirt fabric covering his back and shoulders, emphasizing the strength in their contours. Sierra's fingers almost cramped with wanting to come up behind him and explore in more detail exactly what time and work had done to every muscle.

"That our break-up was inevitable, I guess," he answered. "That we shouldn't blame ourselves…"

"I'm not blaming my—!"

"…or each other," he finished quietly, undercutting her protest. "I'm saying we made clear-sighted choices and those choices weren't compatible, which means that what happened to our marriage was inevitable. Not something to regret. Something to accept. Celebrate, even."

"Celebrate?"

"The fact that when it was good, it was very,

very good, Sierra." His voice communicated the sensuality in his meaning, and memories overtook her in a tidal wave of image and emotion.

All the different ways they'd made love. Hungry to see each other after a busy day apart. Sleepy in the middle of the night. Stretching out every moment during a long seduction that they'd both been planning all week, over a picnic supper on the coffee table in front of a rented movie.

She'd felt sometimes as if they were the king and queen in a magic realm that no-one else even knew existed. She'd felt that if only more people could find what they had, the whole world would be a better place. She'd felt utterly blessed.

"Okay, I won't argue that," she said, instantly breathless.

Yes, their marriage had been good, in so many different ways. So good that it still hurt to think about how far they'd moved away from those times in the years since.

"Can't we celebrate it?" Ty twisted and flattened his palms on the wood of the rail, so that its edge pressed against the small of his back and his silver-gray dress shirt tightened across his chest.

"How?"

By sleeping together? If he was working his

way around to that again, no thanks! The cold awakening afterward couldn't possibly be worth the temporary bliss.

Sierra edged her way to one of the Adirondack chairs that angled to face the vista to the north. Seated, she felt the chair's wooden arms as a protection against the awareness of Ty that seemed so dangerous. Because if he was talking about making love with her…

Oh my, despite all her inner doubts, would she actually possess the emotional strength to resist?

"By respecting each other, over the next few days," he said, and she started to breathe again. "By enjoying the time we spend together. By…" He stopped and sighed tightly between his teeth. "…not hurting each other again, if we can somehow manage that."

"I've never tried or wanted to hurt you, Ty. Never." She sat up straighter. "I've been angry, yes, but I've—"

"Okay. Okay." He gave a quick, jerky nod. "I know. Can't imagine you ever trying to hurt anyone, when I think about it."

"If you want that to sound like a compliment, you'd better try it again." Her mouth felt tight when she'd finished speaking, and she saw him watching her as she consciously tried to let it smooth out.

"It wasn't a compliment or a criticism," he said, after a few seconds. He looked thoughtful and a little more distant suddenly. "It was just an observation." After a second silence, he asked, "Do you want a drink? Hot chocolate? Tea? Something stronger?"

"Tea would be nice." She started to get up, but he lifted his hand. She saw the way his eyes flicked hungrily to her body and then away again.

"Stay. I'll get it." He went inside at once, as if he'd be safer in the kitchen, while Sierra felt that she'd definitely be safer if she stayed out here.

Safe out of his company?

Once upon a time, his body had meant safety to her. In his arms, at seventeen, she'd felt safe and shielded in a way she hadn't since before the frightening onset of her mother's illness. When Ty had left Landerville the shield had gone, and she couldn't for a moment afford the illusion of believing it might be back.

When he brought out her mug of tea she took it from him quickly, taking care that their fingers didn't touch, and as she drank she filled the conversational space with bright, bland little questions about the bird life on the Onslow Banks and whether Cookie was as efficient on a boat as she seemed to be at the front desk.

After ten minutes of this stuff Ty manufactured a convincing yawn, said goodnight and disappeared in the direction of his room, and Sierra tried to push away the senseless flood of disappointment that washed over her. Logic and good sense should never be this hard.

She called Ohio as a way of getting her priorities back in place, but Angie was in a difficult mood because her boyfriend Todd hadn't called when he'd promised to, and it was after eleven, now.

"Can you get off the phone, Sierra? Because you know Dad won't have Call Waiting even though I've begged him, and I'm recharging my cell, and if Todd gets a busy signal… And I'm *not* calling him. I'm not that needy!"

"Wanting me to get off the phone is a little needy, isn't it, Angie?" Sierra suggested gently.

Apparently not.

"We've already talked about, like, fifty-six million times today, you and I," Angie said.

Sierra took a breath, getting ready to point out that most of those times, she wasn't the one who had first picked up the phone to dial. But she

didn't say it in the end, didn't enjoy feeling irri-
table or arguing petty details with her sister like
this. She'd rather be lying in bed—*alone*—listening to the sea.

"Dad's fine," Angie summarized. "Lena's out.
Jordy's staring at his computer."

Sierra sighed. "Okay, Angie, I'll get off the
phone."

She said it and Ty heard it, since he was
standing in the doorway—why had he come
back, he wondered—but he noticed she didn't
actually do it. She was still there several minutes
later, with Angie doing ninety-five percent of the
talking at the other end of the line.

Every now and then, Sierra would get in a supportive line like, "But you knew this was going to
be a difficult time in your relationship." Mostly,
however, the support consisted of listening and
nodding, even though Angie wouldn't be able to
see the nods, and little tongue-clicking sounds and
lip-pressing "mm" sounds that encouraged Angie
to keep spilling whatever was troubling her.

And Ty was so totally torn between wanting to
shake Sierra's shoulders and tell her, "Stop being
so good to them!" and at the same time feeling
almost humbled and in awe about the amount of

warmth and care she displayed, that he just couldn't stay and listen to it any longer.

Sierra hadn't noticed him arrive, and, still focused on her phone call, she didn't notice when he left.

Yeah, they'd done the right thing, not giving into the heat that had overtaken them so power-fully down at the marina when he'd kissed her. He'd lived with coming a distant fifth to Mayor Taylor, Jordy, Angie and Lena for four years. He wasn't going to run that same race all over again.

Maybe it was good that he'd come back to try for a better goodnight with her.

Be honest, Ty, a *hotter* goodnight.

Instead, he'd gotten another reminder that the heat they generated in each other was always the easiest part of what they'd had.

Chapter Five

Ty had left for the marina by the time Sierra woke up the next morning but she found a note in the kitchen, commanding her presence at *Tides* for brunch.

Since it would be petty not to show up just because she didn't care for the nuances of wording in his invitation when being seen with Ty at places like *Tides* was the whole point of her still being here in Stoneport, she called the Garrett Marine office and left a message with Cookie to say that she was on her way in.

When she got there the place was even busier than it had been at lunch-time the previous day.

One class was just going out and a couple of boats were about to leave the dock for their day-long charters. Apparently a couple more had already set sail. Another class had begun to gather, and two Garrett Marine crewmen went back and forth on the dock, checking over the boats and fending off questions.

The questions that Sierra overheard would have sounded more appropriate coming from fans stationed beside the red carpet on Oscar night than from alleged sailing enthusiasts strolling around an Atlantic coast marina. Ty had never looked for that kind of attention or that kind of validation, and she began to understand on a deeper level how much it must be getting to him.

"Is he around, Cookie?" she asked in the office, sounding genuinely like a wife with a harried husband who badly needed her to take him out for a break. She ignored the looks from the two women currently booking a beginner's class for tomorrow.

"He's in the back office taking a radio call from one of our boats," Cookie said. "Might be a problem, I think."

Ty appeared thirty seconds later, and Sierra could see the intent to cancel written on his face even before he spoke. "We have a party in trouble out there," he said, sounding alert and in control but clearly concerned at the same time.

"In the sound, in these conditions?" Sierra said.

The weather was perfect and so was the forecast.

"The husband is having chest pains and the wife is panicking, understandably. It does sound like a heart attack."

"Oh, no!"

"I'm going to get Adam to run me out to them in the power boat. We can bring the husband back in the power boat, and the wife, too, because she probably won't want to leave him, and one of us can sail the other boat in. Cookie, can you call 911 so we'll have an ambulance waiting on the dock when they get here?"

"Gotcha, boss."

"Find out how far away the coast guard is right now, also, just in case. The family has their two teenage boys with them. They can help crew the boat."

"What if they want to go with their Dad, too?" Sierra said.

"I can handle the boat on my own if I have to."

"Let me come with you, Ty."

He flicked a quick look over what she was wearing, then nodded. "Kick those sandals off in my office and grab a pair of deck shoes from the box in the store-room. I'll tell Adam what's happening. Meet me at the power boat—next dock, nearest the board walk—as soon as you can."

"Um, Mr. Garrett?" one of the waiting women said.

"Cookie can handle any questions you have," he answered, cheerful but very firm about it.

And evidently they did have questions, because when Sierra came in from the back office a couple of minutes later, minus her sandals and wearing a pair of deck shoes half a size too big, she heard Cookie say, "Yep, she's his wife. Don't shoot me, ladies, I'm just the messenger." Then when she saw Sierra, she flipped a look across at her and added in a more private aside, "Hope it goes okay. Ty seems pretty laid back about it, but…"

She quirked the corner of her mouth to finish the sentence, and the waiting women looked round-eyed and impressed. They hadn't expected to see their *A-list* hero actually in the process of behaving like one.

The power boat roared out of the marina and into the open expanse of Carteret Sound just minutes later.

"They shouldn't be too hard to find," Ty said.

"He managed to give us a clear indication of his position, although he sounded as if it was an effort."

"Heard anything since?" Adam asked. He was a strong young man in his early twenties, who reminded Sierra a little of her brother Jordy.

"No, but we'll give them a radio call now, let them know our ETA and get an update."

The voice they heard when Ty made the call must belong to one of the man's sons. The teenager sounded tense and upset, and his newly broken voice cracked into a treble more than once. "He says he's not in so much pain any more. He's lying down in the cabin. Mom won't let him move. I think he's worse than he says. Can you get here fast?"

"Should be with you in about ten minutes."

Since the sailboat was hugged fairly close to shore, within the shelter of Carteret Sound, and the swell was low and smooth with only a light, steady wind riffling the water, it was relatively easy to transfer the stricken man to the power boat.

The pain had eased, he reported, "But I feel as weak as a baby." His skin looked clammy, too, and his part in moving from boat to boat had made every limb tremble.

"Do you want me to run you back, sir?" Ty

asked. "Adam is more than up to it, but it's your choice, and my responsibility."

The ill man looked at Adam, then back to Ty. "Sailboat's new this season, isn't it?"

"Yes, you're only the second party to take her out apart from the runs we did ourselves."

"Then you'd better do the important job." He had a twinkle in his eye, even though he spoke with an effort. "Leave us with Adam, here. You take the new boat."

"And I want the boys to come with us, too," his wife declared. Ty didn't argue her out of it.

Sierra wasn't surprised that the family wanted to stay together. Good families tended to work that way. Adam and Ty exchanged a few words, Sierra and Ty moved onto the sailboat, and then the power boat roared away again, back toward the harbor.

"I'm glad you came, Sierra," Ty told her. "Can you grab the tiller and we'll get this baby turned around."

"That's why you're glad I came? So I could steer?"

"Isn't it why you offered?"

Their eyes met and they both laughed, and the memories came flooding in—different memories from the ones that had been so hard on them both last night, but just as powerful.

Replace one large, cold ocean with one small, sunny Ohio lake. Downsize this streamlined thirty-five foot metal and fiberglass craft to a battered little mirror dinghy with a green-painted wooden hull. Finally, strip ten or eleven years worth of life experience from each of them, and you had picture after picture of the summer afternoons they'd spent together on the water.

Ty's love of sailing had been a secret he'd kept from Sierra for the entire first year they'd gone out together, almost as if it was too important to talk about and as if his feelings about it left him vulnerable, although of course he'd never said so.

She'd been surprised to learn that he sailed and that he dreamed of the sea. When had he even seen the Atlantic Ocean? His grandparents certainly couldn't have shown it to him. They almost never left Landerville, let alone Ohio. It had taken Ty a while to fill in this particular piece of the patchwork of his life for Sierra, and even then he'd given her few details.

He'd been fourteen years old, and Mom had come back to town for a visit with a new boyfriend. For once the guy wasn't a total loser. He'd taken them on vacation to the Carolina shore, but Mom, the boyfriend and Ty hadn't meshed too well together. The relationship between the two adults had probably already been breaking down.

The boyfriend had taken Ty out sailing, to escape the bad dynamics. Never talked much, The two of them hadn't ever talked much. They'd let the wind and the water make all the noise, and had just gotten on with the job. For Ty, it had been a window to another world.

His mother had gone back to Los Angeles with the boyfriend after their visit, but they'd split up soon after.

Ty never forgot the water, however, and never lost sight of what he wanted from it—a life, basically. He sweet-talked a neighbor into selling him the old mirror dinghy for twenty-five dollars, and spent most of the next summer scrounging the materials he needed. Not to make it into a flash craft, just to repair it to the point where it wouldn't sink under him like a bathtub with no plug.

"It's a piece of junk," he'd said to Sierra, the first time he'd let her see it. Even then she could see him struggling to hide the pride he couldn't help feeling. "But it gets me from A to A."

"You mean A to B?"

"I mean A to A. Osborne Lake is *round*. And *small*." He'd said each word with a note of disgust. "Can't go anywhere but in a circle, six hundred yards across, and back to where you started from."

And she'd gone in circles with him after that, more times than she could count.

"Remember how to do this?" Ty asked her now, watching her uncertain hand on the tiller.

"I've never done this! Not on a boat like this."

"I guess not. We're not on Osborne Lake any more. Beautiful, isn't she?" He grinned. "Bought her this year, fresh out of the boat yard. I hope our guy's going to be okay. He missed a nice day's sailing, and I could tell he was the type who'd appreciate it, too."

"He looked in better shape than I thought he might."

"We should be able to get a report from the paramedics or the hospital later on. Okay, now you're going to have to duck any second, Sierra, because the boom's about to swing across and I don't want to have to call any more ambulances today."

He gave her orders at approximately thirty second intervals for most of the way back, and when he wasn't ordering, he was telling her,

"That's great, Sierra!" and she couldn't believe how good it felt. When the curve of the shoreline brought them into the lee of the wind, he started up the motor and they put-putted along with less work to do.

Sierra had plenty of time to see how deeply content Ty looked, and how he took in the sight of the sound and the harbor and the waterfront as if every bit of it was his, and he owned heaven.

Sun sparkled on the water and the salt air smelled fresher and better than any fragrance mere money could buy. The marina slid closer and the stone buildings behind it had baked to gold in the spring warmth, like loaves of bread fresh from the oven. They started to hear the familiar music of ropes chinking against metal masts in the wind.

Ty looked just like his picture on the cover of *A-list*. The gold lights in his hair caught the sun, and his eyes were the color of the sea. He should have been grinning, only he clearly felt too lazy to do anything so energetic as that right now. Instead, all the glow came from inside.

"When I look at you here on the water," Sierra said, speaking as the thought formed in her head, "I start to wonder why you even stayed in Landerville as long as you did."

His jaw dropped, his eyes narrowed, he shot her a disbelieving look, and the whole atmosphere between them changed in less than a second, like the sun going behind a dark cloud. Sierra shivered suddenly, as if it actually had.

"You wonder why I stayed?" he echoed. "Don't you *know* why I stayed?" He swore. "Because of you, Sierra. What other reason could there have been?"

"Because of me?"

"We were going out together, remember?" His drawl dripped with sarcasm, like honey dripping from a knife.

He wrenched the tiller toward him as he spoke, starting the tricky maneuver of getting the elegant boat into its mooring. His roughness made the craft turn too sharply and he swore again under his breath as he made a more careful correction.

"Then we had this little wedding thing," he went on, "which—forgive me if I'm being too obvious, here—created this other thing called commitment. Joined lives."

Sierra huffed out a bitter laugh. "You left, Ty. I'm still in Landerville, but you left the whole state, as soon as it suited you, so how can you possibly claim you stayed there because of me?"

He shook his head, frowning at the approaching dock and not looking at Sierra at all.

"Words of one syllable?" he said. "You were in school, then you were in college. Your sisters were still kids, and Jordy not much older. I stayed six years longer than I wanted to. You knew I wanted to start a business, Sierra, and you knew I wanted to work with boats."

Her scalp tightened. So did her throat. He was talking as if they'd had meetings about it, mapped out detailed, practical wish lists and game plans and timetables, but they never had. She was certain they never had. It had been so hard, back then, to get Ty to talk openly and clearly about certain things.

She reminded him, "You went on what you said was a 'fact-finding mission.' First stop Lake Erie."

It hurt to talk, with her throat this tight, and it *really* hurt to yell, but she yelled anyhow, her voice rising higher and louder with every word.

"Next thing I know, I walk in from my summer job and you're home again, talking a mile a minute about selling your grandparents' land to by a rust bucket of a boat rental operation six hundred miles away on the Atlantic coast. It's virtually a done deal, already. You've got realtors working on it, you've talked to the bank, I'm the last person to get told."

"Only because I had to move fast," he yelled back. "Someone else was going to see the same possibilities as I had, if I didn't act."

"You never said you were looking that far away!"

"I did. I talked about the ocean." He didn't look at her, focused intently on the approaching dock. "You just didn't want to hear."

"Because I didn't want to move so far away from my family! I thought you'd take that into consideration."

"I took it into consideration. For six years."

"Families last a life-time, Ty."

"Forgive me but I never realized I'd married five people. I only thought I'd married you. That *we* were the important partnership, the two people whose futures we had to consider."

I never realized I'd married five people.

The words shocked Sierra, and she attacked back without a second's thought.

"You wouldn't have a clue what it's like, would you, to be close to—?" She stopped, horrified at herself.

"No," he agreed, his voice strained. "You're right. I wouldn't know what it's like to be close to a loving family. Thanks for pointing that out. And thanks for attacking me with it, Sierra, as if it's my fault."

The sailboat nudged the dock, Ty jumped to his feet, and somewhere close by a camera clicked and clicked and clicked. Startled by it and burning with regret, throat still painful from yelling, Sierra looked across and recognized the photographer from the local paper, who'd taken their picture for the social pages just last night.

He had a satisfied expression on his face, and a set of very different shots of Ty and Sierra Garrett in his camera this morning. Too late, she realized that he wouldn't have been the only person to hear the two of them arguing on the boat, either.

"Hey, Matt," Ty said, the casual greeting forced. He'd already roped the boat to the dock. Now, without waiting for Sierra, he leaped across the undulating gap between deck and dock and walked toward the other man.

"Ty," the photographer answered. He looked a little uncomfortable.

"What's this about?"

"For a colleague. She wanted some, uh, shots of the waterfront, some of the action at Garrett Marine."

There'd be some action in those pictures, all right, Sierra knew. Angry gestures. Screwed up faces. Flaming looks. Unmistakable body language. With the right caption, the pictures could be used as evidence of whatever a journalist wanted—a marriage on the rocks, a successful businessman with a much darker side, financial problems within Garrett Marine.

Unless the motivation for getting the pictures was personal.

"She?" Ty said. "Lucy Little?"

"Uh, yes, from *A-list*. She's very successful, you obviously know that, and very well-respected."

"Is she paying you?"

Matt colored, and muttered something about a professional favor.

"Well, I'm not paying you, either," Ty said, "but I want those pictures. This isn't journalism, Matt, and you know it. It's gossip. I thought your ambitions were cleaner and better than that."

Somehow, Ty already had the digital camera out of Matt's hand, and his fingers moved over it with as much confidence as his body moving around a boat. "Okay, they're deleted," he said after a few moments.

"What am I going to tell her?"

"Tell her you had your thumb over the lens." He turned. "Sierra, *sweetheart,* are you ready for brunch, now? Later than we planned, I know…"

Brunch? She was ready to get in the car and drive back to Ohio. Did he really want to go on with this? That "sweetheart" of his had sounded so cutting she wanted to check her body for blood.

Ty stepped toward her and before she knew what was happening her chin was locked onto his shoulder, her body was locked in his arms and he was whispering in her ear. "I know. You want to high-tail it out of here as fast as the North Carolina state speed limit permits. But do you really want us to separate in bitterness and anger *again?* How much of a failure would that seem to both of us, the second time around?"

Chapter Six

"No, okay, you're right. I—I guess I don't want to part in anger again," Sierra answered Ty at last, and he slowly let out the breath he'd unconsciously been holding.

"Good," he said. He didn't let her see how badly he'd wanted her agreement. "It's eleven and I'm starving. I'm going to get Denny or Cookie to tie down the boat while we eat."

He didn't know why it was so important that she stay. It was about more than just tying up the loose ends and not parting in anger, although those things were definitely a factor.

Was it true that he'd never articulated his real

ambitions clearly enough for her to understand either what they were or how much they mattered? He always thought they'd had good lines of communication going between them.

Apparently she didn't agree, however, and they should explore that.

In the office, he called the local hospital and learned that their probable heart attack case had arrived safely and would be undergoing some tests soon. The good news added an extra note of optimism to his already strong determination that the day should go in a positive rather than a negative direction.

When he and Sierra reached *Tides,* Gina asked him, "Usual table?"

"Please, if it's free."

"And move the ship?" She was talking about the model boat they'd used as a screen yesterday.

"Just keep the ship moved for the next couple of weeks, Gina," he told her, "if it doesn't make it too awkward for you guys to reach the other tables."

"Well, table twelve's a little problematic but we manage so don't worry about it."

"Thanks!"

"Do you really need to care about your staff bumping their hips on the tables?" Sierra asked, when they were seated and on their own. "That level of detail, when you're the owner and CEO of Garrett Marine?"

"I've waited quite a few tables in my time," he reminded her, hearing how stiff and prickly his tone came out. "No need for me to get a convenient attack of amnesia about the challenges of the job, now that I've moved up in the world."

She nodded but didn't say anything, and he wondered if he'd sounded self-righteous on the subject. He hadn't meant to. One of the challenges of owning a business empire was how to retain the right authority while showing an appreciation for your staff. He let the issue go when Sierra spoke.

"There must be other places to eat in this town, that aren't owned by Garrett Marine," she said.

"I tried that. But then I didn't even have the staff on side about the *A-list* thing, and it was worse." He took a slow breath. "Did you mean everything you said, back on the boat?"

She colored at once. "No. No, I didn't!" She took his hand across the table, and the warm contact arrowed direct to his groin, just as it had last night, just as his body wanted. "I never should have said that thing about loving families, Ty. It was…unforgivable, really. I—"

"True, though."

"Not even that. You did have a loving relationship with your grandmother, even though I know she was—"

"So vague and eccentric that she hardly knew what day of the week it was," he supplied the blunt wording for her.

"—and I wish I could have met her."

"It wasn't the same. You don't have to tell me. Even at our best, the Garretts were pretty dysfunctional. What I meant was, do you really feel that I didn't tell you what my ambitions were?"

She gave him a helpless look and turned her hand palm upward—the hand that wasn't still pressed over his, creating havoc. "We talked about climbing mountains in Africa, Ty, and seeing the midnight sun in Norway. Having twelve children and sailing the world, homeschooling them on board the boat."

"You remember that one?"

"And I remember the one about starting a free learn-to-sail program on Osborne Lake for disadvantaged kids."

"Yeah, I liked that one." He smiled. "I still think about that one, sometimes."

"Oh, you do?"

"It would be great to do something like that here, under the umbrella of Garrett Marine."

"And do you remember the one about running a catering company that delivered gourmet picnic orders to campers in state parks?"

"That was a little more problematic," he said. "I doubt we'd have gotten a business loan for that one."

"You see, Ty? We were kids who thought we had the world at our feet just because we were together."

"Yeah, we did, didn't we?"

"We had a million different ideas, and we laughed about most of them a week after we'd come up with them. How was I supposed to know, out of all that, which was the thing you really meant to do?"

"I guess the thing I really meant to do was the one I was too scared to talk about much," he answered, "in case the Garrett family's out-of-touch-with-reality jinx kicked in. My mom used to tell me over and over about how it would be when she was a world-famous recording artist, as if it was a bed-time fairy tale."

"And it turned out to be just that? A fairy tale?"

"Right. Exactly. You know, when a parent

makes such huge mistakes, you bend over backward not to follow in the same footsteps."

"I should have seen that about you. I should have looked deeper."

"No. You had four other people to be wise and perceptive about, and three of them were kids. You shouldn't have had to act like a parent with me as well, interpreting my adolescent moods. But I couldn't see that back then."

"There were a few things we couldn't see about each other, I guess," she agreed in a careful voice. "Or about ourselves. You were right in what you said on the boat. You didn't marry five people. I— I need to think about that."

"Ready to order?" Gina said, bouncing up to their table.

They hadn't even opened their menus. Ty looked at his and felt helpless. Sierra took her hand away and he wanted to grab it back.

Gina took pity on both of them. "Have the special," she said.

"What is it?"

"Brioche, Italian ham, all sorts of stuff. You liked it last week."

"What, you guys take notes about my preferences, in there?"

"Keepin' the boss happy." She grinned, looking pretty happy herself. So maybe he hadn't been self-righteous about considering the placement of the tables, earlier.

"Okay, I'll have the special," he said. "With coffee."

"Me, too," Sierra said.

Gina was bouncing again before she'd even finished noting their order, and he had to ask, "Having a good day?"

Gina almost blushed. "There have been certain flow-on benefits out of the *A-list* story, actually."

"Yeah?"

"It's complicated. I met someone. Came to Stoneport in search of his ex-girlfriend, who'd come in search of the Bachelor of the Year. Cutting to the punch-line for you, now, he decided I was more interesting than the ex-girlfriend. So I owe you, boss." She beamed, and headed for the kitchen.

"See?" Sierra said. "A waterfront dating agency. I thought of it yesterday. You'd be raking it in."

"Another ambition neither of us is serious about."

Her voice dropped. "I get it now, Ty, okay? I was unfair. The whole argument was unfair and unfortunately it got overheard. Do you think deleting the photos is going to be enough?"

"Come sailing courtesy of Garrett Marine on Friday. Along with our dinner at the mayor's tonight, that should repair the damage. I have a full-day picnic charter cruise to take out. Eight women from New Jersey, plus the father of one of them, who's seventy-five."

"Yes, I can see where he would need me as a chaperone, in that situation," she nodded, mock serious, and they laughed about a whole lot of things for most of the way through their meal.

Sierra spent another afternoon relaxing on Ty's deck and walking on the beach. Having his large, well-appointed yet homey place to herself felt like being in paradise and she realized what a rare treat it was.

At home, there were always people coming and going. Her own friends with their relationship problems or their cute babies and new-parent fatigue. Lena's serial dates. Jordy's buddies behaving like a pack of wolf cubs. Dad's business contacts and his associates in civic affairs. Even when the house was quiet, she never knew how long it would last, and she mostly used the window of time to tackle her share of the household chores.

After brunch this morning, however, Ty had told her that he wouldn't be home until six-thirty this evening, ready to change for their dinner with Stoneport's mayor at seven, so she knew she had an uninterrupted stretch of time to herself in a place that was already immaculate.

She was even tempted to turn down the volume on Ty's answer-machine and switch off her cell, but didn't in the end. A couple of calls from home wouldn't ruin this delectable sense of peace and freedom.

It passed too quickly, punctuated by cool drinks on the deck, a sandwich snack, and a run through her exercise routine—with music in the background—which she neglected far too often at home.

As expected, Lena did call—twice—but that was okay.

"I really, really appreciate you when you're not around, Sierra, I'm telling you!" she said. "You are just the best!"

Ty got home a little later than he'd wanted to and Sierra had been relying on his arrival to keep her on schedule so they both had to scramble to get ready in time. She'd taken a spa bath after her exercise, complete with drops of aromatherapy oil in the water, so at least there was no need to shower.

The second dress she'd bought yesterday was a simple ankle-length sheath in midnight blue silk velour. With a modest split at the side, it hugged her figure and fell just right without needing to be ironed, its rich color brightened with the addition of a shimmering wrap in an electric royal blue. She folded her hair in its usual work-day French pleat, kept her make-up simple, and managed to arrive in Ty's living room just half a minute after he did.

"Perfect, again," he told her.

Should she appreciate a compliment like this?

Somehow, she didn't. After the way they'd connected this morning over their brunch, she'd wanted something more personal, something that wasn't just about the performance he wanted her to act out as his wife. She didn't allow herself to explore the sense of disappointment too deeply, though, and took care to focus on the drive.

Mayor John Caldwell and his wife Ruth lived in an elegant brick townhouse in Stoneport's street of beautifully preserved historic mansions, dating from the hey-day of shipping trade with the West Indies nearly two hundred years ago. The neighborhood reminded Sierra of the houses she'd seen in Washington, D.C.'s Georgetown area, while on a field trip she'd made there with her fifth grade class two years ago.

She wasn't surprised when Ty told her, as he parked out front, "John has big political ambitions. He's hoping to run for Congress in a few years and I think he has a good shot at success. He has a high profile around here, as well as popularity and some influential friends."

"The CEO of Garrett Marine being one of them?" She looked up at him as he opened the passenger door for her.

"He seems to think so." Ty grinned, then added, "No, he's a nice guy. We wouldn't be friends if he wasn't."

He adjusted her wrap for her, the brush of his fingers echoing the soft touch of the floaty fabric, and the movements he made felt too intimate and too nice on her relaxed and recharged body. Inhaling, she smelled the sweet fragrance of the bath oil rising from her skin's clean pores, and instinctively closed her eyes when Ty bent from behind and let his cheek nuzzle her neck.

"Just in case someone's watching from the window," he murmured, and reality kicked in again like a shower of cold rain blowing in from the ocean.

Ruth Caldwell opened the door almost before the echo of the bell had died away. She was an attractive woman in her early forties, with a natural-looking beauty that would allow her to flirt a little as well as behaving with maternal sternness when she chose to—and she chose to right away.

"So, tell us exactly how and why you haven't said anything before, Ty!" she said, raising her eyebrows and flicking her gaze from Ty to Sierra and back again.

"I guess it would be superfluous at this point to make a formal introduction," he drawled. "But this is Sierra, my wife."

Ruth drew Sierra into her arms for a quick but sincere hug. "Sierra, honey, it's great to meet you, even if we didn't know you existed until Ty called us yesterday and asked us—far too casually, I might say!—if we could add his *wife* to our guest list."

"It's great to meet you, too," Sierra said.

"Can we leave it at that for the moment, Ruth?" Ty asked. "If Sierra and I go into the nitty gritty details here in the hallway, we'll only have to repeat it over dinner, won't we? Are Lisa and Paul coming tonight?"

"They are."

"And Harry and Tarsha?"

"And Bill and Jade, and an older couple you don't know, Don and Renee. But that's it, I promise."

"Not Alicia?"

"No. She cancelled…"

"Right." He didn't seem particularly disappointed to hear the news.

Ruth made a significant face. "…when she found out that you, uh, weren't coming alone. Sierra, honey, you've disappointed a few women in this town." She added quickly, "But you're right, Ty, let's leave the hot topic until everyone can hear about it at the same time."

"We're not the first?"

"No, but you're not the last, either."

"Harry and Tarsha?"

"As usual. They're going to have to stop blaming the baby, soon. She's nearly four years old!"

Sierra laughed, and Ruth threw her an approving look, which set the tone for the whole evening, in contrast to those awkward few moments following the mention of another woman's name. These were lovely people—successful and well-situated, but not pretentious or judgmental. As Ty had said, he wouldn't have been friends with them if they had been.

They stood in a spacious formal sitting room

for drinks and appetizers, and every time someone asked about the past that Ty and Sierra shared, Ruth sternly told them to wait until dinner was served.

Sierra felt grateful for her intervention until, inevitably, they all sat down at the rosewood dining table, and dinner *was* served, and everyone fell into an expectant silence over their linguine and white clam sauce as soon as Tarsha leaned forward and asked encouragingly, "Well, you two? Spill!"

"Whole story?" Ty said.

"Just try cutting corners on any of it and see what happens!"

"We've been married for twelve years," he began, and everyone gasped.

"You must have been babies!" Ruth said.

"Eighteen and twenty."

"As I said, babies."

"So you won't be surprised to hear that after I moved here from Ohio and we tried to keep up a long distance relationship because of Sierra's commitments at home, we couldn't make it work." He turned to Sierra, seated beside him on his right, and gave her a rueful, dewy-eyed, cute-puppy look as he placed his hand on her knee. "Could we, darling?"

"Um, no." With that very un-Ty-like look on his face, she wanted to slap his hand away, despite the thrills of warm sensation running all the way up her thighs. His easy mingling of truth and what-might-have-been confused her, and she didn't know how to react.

Her body knew, of course, but she wasn't taking any notice of such traitorous input as that.

"So what happened, Ty," Bill Sorensen said. "Because you're obviously together again, now."

"Time happened, I guess," Ty answered. "Some growing up, some thinking, a couple of meetings away from day-to-day pressure to talk through the issues—the *A-list* article acted as a bit of a catalyst, of course—and we've decided to have a second try. Which should be easier, given that we never officially got divorced."

He was clever, Sierra had to give him that. He'd picked exactly the right places to stick to the facts, while still creating the rosy impression of their future which he was so eager to spread around town.

Bill Sorensen was a senior officer at the nearby marine corps base. Paul and Lisa owned a successful construction company with branches in Wilmington, Jacksonville and Myrtle Beach. Tarsha was a former model, while her husband Harry maintained a luxury home here as their weekend and vacation escape from his growing computer software business in Raleigh. Along with the mayor and his wife, they were people who would be listened to, and this was what Ty wanted.

By the time it became apparent that their "second try" had failed, the heat over the *A-list* story would have faded and they could get their overdue divorce in peace. It was all so neat and believable that Ty's hand on her knee, and his shoulder pressing closer against hers, and that sweet, vulnerable, love-struck look in his eye were all totally unnecessary.

So she trod on his foot.

"That's adorable!" Renee said. "I wish my daughter and her ex could have had the same vision and the same commitment. They gave up at the first hurdle."

"I'm not a man who gives up easily," Ty answered.

He neatly flipped his foot out from under Sierra's and away from him, so that it came to rest beside her instep, leaving the inner side of her calf pressed against his in a twisted sheath of silk velour and masculine suit fabric.

"And that's what I don't see in too many men

these days," said Renee's husband Don. "The tenacity. The vision."

"Yes, it's so vital to know exactly where you want to go, isn't it?" Ty agreed.

And where he wanted to go was up his wife's legs, apparently.

His hand was sliding higher, slipping off her knee and around to the soft inner skin of her thigh, taking full advantage of the knee-high split in the side of her dress, and since his broad foot was in between her shoes, now, she couldn't snap her legs together the way she wanted to…no, correction, *didn't* want to, if she was honest about it, didn't want to for a second.

Sigh.

Across the table, she saw a knowing twinkle appear in Ruth Caldwell's eye. "It's pretty easy to see where you two are going," she said. "And as Renee says, it's adorable. I love it. So life-affirming."

"John, I guess Ty told you that my father is mayor in my hometown, right?" Sierra said quickly. Turning toward him with the question, she was able to disguise the moment when she successfully wrenched her leg off the top of Ty's and back under her own control.

"Yes, for quite some time, now, I under-stand," he said.

"Eighteen years."

"He doesn't hanker for a role on a bigger stage?"

"No, he doesn't. He's very community-minded. I think he'd lose everything he loves about his role if he took it to the next level."

"And you think it's good for the town to have the same person at the helm of local affairs for so long?"

"When it's a man like my dad, yes, absolute-ly," Sierra answered with both spirit and charm, then went on to argue a convincing case.

Listening to her, Ty repented of the way he'd tried to play footsie with her a few moments ago. She was doing this for him, the way she always did things for other people, and he should be grateful for that, not making it harder for her than it needed to be.

He shouldn't be making it harder for himself, either. He knew that the chemical heat between them wasn't the true barrier they couldn't get past, and he knew it didn't have the power to make everything right.

There was so much more to their relationship than that. She was fully aware of it, and she could re-think her willingness to help him out at any time.

On the subject of helping him out, just how many of their complicated interactions over the past two days were really about cooling the gossip? At heart, he knew that there was so much more going on. He needed to be honest with himself about it, he needed to work out what he wanted, and what was possible.

And he needed to do it soon, he knew, or his chance would be gone and he doubted it would ever come again.

Chapter Seven

"**H**oney, if you've e-mailed him and text messaged him and spoken to his room-mate and left two messages on his voice mail, then you just have to wait until he has a chance to call," Sierra said into the phone as Ty entered his living room on Thursday evening, her dark eyes serious. She listened for a moment and he saw her front teeth scrape across her full lower lip.

She had to be speaking to one of her sisters again. Angie, apparently, since they were covering pretty much the same ground as they had when he'd overheard a part of their conversation on Tuesday night. Ty could summarize it in three words after overhearing just eight seconds of speech.

Todd hadn't called.

He put down a briefcase full of spreadsheet print-outs and contemplated his future. His immediate future, to be more specific. Shower, eat, drink or talk to Sierra? His body felt sticky with fatigue, his stomach was like an empty cave since he'd only managed to grab a muffin and coffee at *Tides* for lunch, he was thirsty—water or beer, he'd take either—and he knew he'd left his wife too much to her own devices today.

It was past eight in the evening, and after taking out a morning charter cruise because Matt was off sick, and conducting a scheduled two-hour sailing class this afternoon, he was way behind with administrative stuff and later in getting home than he'd intended.

Almost hidden behind the stacks of papers on his desk at the main office, he'd snatched a moment to call the hospital at around four to check once again on yesterday's heart attack guy, who was resting comfortably, he was told, and would be discharged tomorrow. He would need routine by-pass surgery in his home town soon. Ty had also called Sierra, here at the house, but she hadn't picked up so he'd just left a message warning her he wouldn't be home until around seven.

An optimistic prediction, as it had turned out.

Apparently she wasn't angry about it, however. She waved at him and managed to smile even while she also kept nodding and listening and making those supportive "mm" noises, then said into the phone, "Angie, wait until you hear what he has to say, and stay calm about it or you will sound needy, okay?"

Deciding on a glass of water, followed by a shower, Ty went into the kitchen and discovered that she'd cooked. He probably would have smelled the delectable aroma escaping the oven as soon as he'd entered the house, except that Sierra had his deck doors wide open again and the fresh salt breeze coming across the dunes over-powered everything else.

Peering through the oven's glass front, he saw something creamy steaming away in a round cas-serole dish, and identified chunks of chicken and mushroom and vegetable. Another casserole dish held a fluffy heap of white rice, set in the oven to keep warm, and his stomach flipped and growled at the very thought of piling the food on his plate.

Okay, he decided as he gulped the glass of

water, he'd make it a quick shower, so the meal didn't spoil.

On his way back through the living room and up the stairs, he heard Sierra again.

"How many times did you check it today?" She listened for a moment. "Oh, he did?" She sounded pleased, but then her voice fell again. "Oh, he said he *would*."

Apparently that wasn't such good news.

"Well, did he? Did you ask? Please ask, Angie, and get the numbers, and get him to call me— him, not you—if he wasn't within the normal range. I don't care if it's late. Just whenever he gets home, I want him to call. I know you're distracted because Todd hasn't called but— Yes, I know. I know. Okay. Love you, too."

Her voice faded as Ty reached his bedroom.

After a two minute shower, he came down again and asked her, "Don't they drive you nuts?" He didn't need to specify who he meant.

"Yes." She shrugged and smiled, quirking the corner of her expressive mouth. "But they left me alone all afternoon, which is better than yesterday."

"What did you do?"

"Absolutely nothing. Until I started cooking. I loved every second of it."

"The cooking?"

"The nothing. If you didn't allegedly need me to defend your seventy-five-year-old client against all those assertive younger women on the boat tomorrow, I might have opted for more of the same."

"More nothing? Get real!" he teased her. "The Sierra Taylor I've known for fourteen years? Four days in a row containing big chunks of nothing? I bet you haven't done that since you used to lie in your crib looking at a string of rattles stretched across the top, and I don't believe you could do another day of it if you tried."

"You can stretch a string of rattles across your deck rail for me, if you like, and I promise I'll look at them for hours at a time."

Smiling again, she raised her hands behind her head and arched her back. He heard a couple of joints crack, which made her smile wider, and he realized her mouth hadn't done that sucking on a lemon thing in his presence in two days. She looked so beautiful and graceful when she stretched.

And she really needed this break. Couldn't her family see that? Couldn't they be generous enough not to tell her they loved her quite so often, so sincerely and so needfully?

"You don't have to come sailing," he told her.

"I'll arm the old man with some pepper spray and I'm sure he'll be able to fight the women off."

"You know that's not why I'm going sailing."

"Yes, I know that's not why you're going sailing. But the real reason isn't totally urgent, either. We've been seen by plenty of people since Tuesday."

"Arguing loudly, at one point."

"Which is exactly what most married couples do."

"We didn't used to. Not seriously. Only that one time, before you left."

"Maybe if we'd argued more we would have known more about what each other was thinking."

She shrugged as if she didn't like this idea.

"Have you decided yet how long you're staying?" he asked.

This time, she sighed and made a helpless sound. "No. I'm— I mean— Sometimes I think I could do with a whole— No."

"No hurry," he answered mildly.

"To decide, or to leave?"

Either.

Right now, he wasn't pushing her about either.

And he got the uncomfortable feeling that each of them was waiting for something, some defining statement from the other person about the past or the future. He just didn't know what that statement was.

They suffered all through the delicious meal she'd cooked, pretending they weren't flaming with their awareness of each other, and he left her with a pile of videos and went back into town for another couple of hours' work after they'd eaten, because he didn't trust what he might do if he stayed.

"I'm so excited!" announced the Woman Who Loved Sailor Suits Too Much—the one Sierra had first encountered on Tuesday.

Today's selection looked like a 1940's Hollywood costume designer's vision for the chorus line in a Fred and Ginger movie, including a sailor hat with a navy pompom. The only thing missing, Sierra decided, was the tap shoes. The thick-soled, over-engineered athletic footwear that Ms Sailor Suit wore instead looked so state-of-the-art that a professional basketball player would have gone for a simpler pair.

Ms Sailor Suit tripped on their bulk just as she reached the waiting sailboat and if Sierra hadn't grabbed her arm she would have landed half in the water, half on the deck, and probably broken something. Or possibly gotten dragged to the bottom of the harbor by the weight of the shoes.

"Thanks!" she gasped.

"No problem, um… Do tell me your name. I'm Sierra." Because I can't keep calling you Ms Sailor Suit, and you're probably a great person, if you would just take a very good friend with you when you're buying your vacation clothes.

Sierra herself had put on calf-length navy capri pants this morning, teaming them with a white tank top that had a built-in bra, as well as sunglasses, a red baseball cap and the last sputtering squirt of her sunblock.

"And I'm Ginger," the other woman answered.

Oh.

Good.

That's going to help.

Ty stood on the deck, waiting to assist the sailor and her suit on board. His eyes locked with Sierra's for a moment and he mouthed, "Whoa!" He'd obviously picked up on the uncanny correlation between Ginger's name and today's fashion influences, even though it seemed that Ginger herself remained unaware.

Sierra grinned back at him, but then three staff from *Nautilus* arrived with the gourmet picnic hampers that had been prepared in the restaurant kitchen, the other women wanted to know where they should put their jackets and bags, and the seventy-five-year-old needed help getting aboard, so she and Ty didn't have the chance to talk.

As it turned out, this didn't seem to matter. Her sense of relaxed connection with him survived the morning's competing distractions. One woman got seasick as soon as they'd nosed beyond the end of the marina. She had to be settled in the cabin below deck while she waited for her motion sickness medication to take effect.

Another two women wanted the champagne opened immediately, although it was only ten in the morning, and Sierra had to wonder whether Ty's catering crew would have supplied enough of the stuff, at this rate. The seventy-five-year-old was keen to show off his sailing skills, but unfortunately he didn't have any and he almost knocked Ginger out cold when he winched the wrong sheet and let the boom swing wildly across the deck.

"Typical day on the water?" Sierra finally got the chance to ask Ty, after a couple of hours, below deck and out of earshot of his paying clients.

"We do get a broad sampling of what human

nature has to offer," he murmured, leaning closer than he strictly needed to, for her to hear. The boat moved quietly when it was under sail. His T-shirt sleeve didn't have to brush her bare shoulder like that. And the hard curve of muscle beneath the sleeve definitely didn't.

"In that sense, it's a lot like teaching," she answered, trying not to think about the sleeve and the muscle, "and I've always loved that aspect of the job."

"Same here. No two days are the same. And I like the way people surprise us, too." He dropped his voice a little more. "Look at Ginger, there, winding that winch. She'd be a natural if she took a few lessons, or found some friends to crew with, and she's having a blast."

"She is, isn't she?"

"I wouldn't have guessed from looking at her. Or rather, her outfit."

"No, you're right. Neither would I. I would have put her down for either the champagne or the seasickness. So this is why you still come out on the water? Because people surprise you? You could easily delegate these picnic cruises to your staff, right?"

"I like to keep personally involved with everything that Garrett Marine does. I never miss an opening at the gallery, and I eat at *Nautilus* and *Crow's Nest* and *Tides* at least once a week. To see friends and regulars and genuine clients, though, not to be chief clown in a media circus."

"No, I can see that."

"It's not an easy distinction to make, at the moment, so if I haven't said it enough yet, thanks for sticking around and helping everyone get it clear."

He put a hand over hers, and she felt the way their forearms brushed together. The moment didn't last but it surprised her with its feeling of intimacy and heat all the same. She saw one of the champagne women eyeing her coolly over the top of another fizzing flute of liquid, and felt as if a very private moment had just been invaded.

Ty went back on deck and Sierra heard him announce, "We'll be dropping anchor in around twenty minutes. Ginger, want to drive this thing for a bit, while we get ourselves through the inlet to the sound?"

The champagne woman's look chilled a little more now that Ty had gone. "Sierra, right?" she said. The level of liquid in the flute dropped a full inch when she took what was intended to look like a dainty sip.

"That's me," Sierra said.

"First I heard a rumor that you and Ty were married, and I guess that has to be true, since you're here. Then I heard a rumor that your marriage is on the rocks. Are you trying for a reconciliation, or something?"

The woman's direct approach had Sierra grabbing blindly for an answer that fell somewhere between the truth and what she knew Ty would want her to say.

"Reconciliation?" she echoed finally. "There's no need for that. You shouldn't listen to rumors, you should judge for yourself."

"Sounds like a challenge, to me."

"It wasn't meant to be."

But Sierra realized too late that she'd set herself up. She was going to get judged for the rest of the day, if she hadn't been judged already. Not something she could look forward to. She'd been looking forward to some quality time with Ty, instead.

Looking forward to it far too much, when she thought about it.

* * *

Ty loved this sheltered spot, located in a secret reach of Carteret Sound. He often brought picnic cruises here, and clients would be happy to linger for two or three hours over their gourmet lunch, swimming and fishing off the boat, walking the sandy shore or just lazing in the sun.

Surveying today's group as they ate, he saw that sure enough they looked happy. Seasickness medication had started working, and champagne wasn't flowing any more freely than it should. Ginger had taken off the athletic shoes that looked more like big white bricks and borrowed a pair of deck shoes from his store of old canvas things with holes. A couple of her toes peeked out of the holes and looked a lot pinker and happier than they would have been when entombed inside the bricks.

The only person who didn't seem happy was Sierra, which was a pity, because she was the one whose state of mind Ty cared about most. She'd kept very busy for the past hour, serving up the picnic, keeping drinks filled, and listening to the old man's tall stories about his past.

But whenever Ty caught her at an unguarded moment, she looked tense—her face, and those bare, tanned shoulders that kept drawing his gaze.

He didn't get a chance to ask her about it until the rest of the group had split up to pursue their chosen activities before it was time to head back.

"What's the problem, Sierra?" She had begun to pack up the remnants of the lunch, stepping warily around the three oil-slicked bodies stretched out in various places on the deck.

"Oh, does it show?" she said.

"That you're tense, yes. Were you hoping it didn't?"

"I don't mind you picking up on it, but if the champagne connoisseur tanning herself up near the bow has intercepted the signals, she's probably taken notes."

"Notes?"

"Just remembering Matt and the camera yesterday, hoping she's not another friend of your *A-list* reporter."

"You think it's possible?"

"She asked me a couple of things, and I got the impression she was pretty thick-skinned about what I might dish out in reply."

She shrugged her bare shoulders and Ty wanted to touch them, test the temperature of her skin to make sure she wasn't getting burned. The sheen of her sun lotion had faded since this morning. He suspected that if he did touch her, however, he'd be the one to feel the fire.

"You know, I just had the feeling that she's used to asking invasive questions," she finished.

"And you think Lucy Little's hoping for a nice, gossipy kicker to her original story, so she's sent a spy?"

"That, or what she said the other day at the café. The personal angle."

"And you want to keep me for yourself."

"Smile when you say that, so that I don't slap you for being serious." She smiled at him to show that she wasn't serious, either. "You *want* me to act as if I want to keep you for myself, remember? It's the whole reason I'm here."

"But you're not comfortable lying about it."

"No. I'm not."

"I'll try to run some interference for you, then. Keep her so busy she doesn't have time to watch us both and wait for cracks opening up."

"That would help."

"Go take a walk on the beach for now, until we have to leave. Cool off in the water on the way."

"Mm, sounds great."

Her expression softened at once, and Ty remembered so clearly the satisfaction he'd felt back in Ohio whenever he was able to lighten her load. She wouldn't let him do it all that often. She wasn't very good at delegating, although he didn't think she knew that. He used to have to trick her—gentle, well-intentioned trickery, but trickery all the same.

He remembered keeping close tabs on their domestic paper-work, making sure he got in before her to pay bills or run errands or whatever, and he remembered the surprised way her face would light up later on when he'd tell her, "Already taken care of."

It was the look any other woman might have given when a man presented her with a bunch of flowers or a piece of jewelry she wasn't expecting, which was…kind of sad, now that he thought about it. He'd been too budget-conscious back then to surprise her with actual gifts.

Had he *ever* given her anything like jewelry or flowers? It didn't take him long to realize that he hadn't.

When it was almost time to head back, Ms Champagne stretched herself and sat up, her tan gleaming. Lowering her sunglasses, she took a good look around and saw Sierra splashing through the shallows back out to the boat in her swimsuit, along with Ginger and a couple of the other women, but then her gaze fixed on Ty and stayed there.

He waved.

Ms Champagne waved back. What was her name? He tried to remember clients' names, but this one wouldn't stick. Sh-something. Cherelle? He thought so.

He beckoned, and she climbed around the mast stays toward him.

"Want to learn something about boats?" he asked.

"I'd rather learn something about boat skippers."

"You have to sign up for that particular class back at our office, and I believe it's already full for this week."

"Tell me the real story, Ty."

"That is the real story. Most of our classes are full, right now."

"About you and Sierra."

And suddenly he couldn't think of any reason not to tell her, so he did, as briefly as possible. "We got married a long time ago and had a few problems. That's why she wasn't around when your friend wrote her article."

Yep, Cherelle's eyes had widened and her

breath had drawn in just a little too sharply. Sierra was right, she was here on Lucy's behalf. She said half-heartedly, "My friend?" but she knew he'd blown her cover, and she didn't try very hard.

"But we've discovered we want to try and work things out," he continued. "So I would really appreciate it if you would tell Lucy, and the entire *A-list* staff if that's necessary, to please respect our privacy and leave us alone, whether this latest bout of interest is professional or personal."

"Well, it's a bit of both, if you want—"

"No, you're not getting it, Cherelle. Listen. I don't care which it is. I just want it to stop."

She nodded, narrowing her intelligent light blue eyes. "Right. Okay. I'll pass that on."

"Good. I appreciate it."

Cherelle left him alone after this, and he had the rest of the trip back to think about what he'd said—that he and Sierra had discovered they wanted to work things out. Just a neat sound bite, put together for public consumption?

No, shoot…damn it…it was true.

True for him, anyhow, if not for Sierra. She didn't have the same demons chasing her that he did. She was stubborn, but he doubted she was as stubborn as he was.

His whole childhood had felt like one long series of defeats. He didn't want to add divorce to the pile, like some final piece of highly combustible fuel, before he set a match to his past and burned it to ash.

No matter how crazy it looked on paper, no matter what his lawyer might say to him on the subject, no matter that he had no strategies in place for convincing Sierra to see things the way he did, he knew he just wasn't ready, yet, to let his marriage go.

Chapter Eight

Sierra had come into Stoneport with Ty in his old sedan this morning, so when they arrived back at the dock after the long, lazy picnic cruise, she didn't have a vehicle.

"Which means you're chained to my schedule, unfortunately," Ty told her as they walked along the dock. "Sorry, I should have thought ahead. I have calls to make at the main office, accounts to go over. Three or four hours work, probably. I can run you out to the house first, if you want."

"Is there something I can help you with, that'll speed things up?" she asked. "I guess since I cooked last night, we're doing feeding time at the zoo again tonight, so…"

She couldn't quite keep the reluctance out of her voice. She really didn't relish the thought of another evening of pretence—pretending to other people that she cared for Ty, while pretending to him and to herself that she didn't. What was the truth, beneath all of that? What really counted for something?

"Feeding time at the zoo?" Ty repeated.

She shrugged and managed to smile. "Eating in public. Getting seen. Acting married."

"You know what?" he said, after a moment. "Let's not. Last night was nice."

"I'll cook again, then, sure."

"Tempting, but no, how about I barbecue on the deck?"

"Hey, we could call up the local TV news, get them to send their helicopter crew to cover the story. An aerial view."

"Or we could not. We could keep it totally private." He brushed his fingers lightly across her cheek and down to her shoulder, making her melt. "I like that plan better."

"So do I," she answered.

Ty delegated Adam to unpack and tie down the

boat, checked in with Cookie, then drove the short distance to his main office with Sierra. Her inadequate squirt of sunblock had worn away during her swim, so she'd gotten a little burned across her shoulders and upper chest, and she felt sleepy, too, after so much sun. In Ty's office, someone brought her a coffee and that woke her up enough to perform a couple of token tasks that he gave her.

Finished with those in less than half an hour, she thought about asking him for something else, but then she remembered Wednesday's conversation about all the plans and ambitions the two of them had once had, and suddenly she was smiling.

"Is there a spare computer and printer I could use for the next couple of hours?" she asked one of Ty's office staff. "Somewhere quiet? With a phone and a local business directory?"

"Sure, in the copy room. You might get a couple of people coming in to use the copier, would that bother you?"

"No, it's fine."

As long as Ty doesn't see what I'm doing until I'm finished…

It was almost six by the time he came looking

for her, just as she'd begun to print out what she'd been working on.

"What's this?" he said. "Not the filing and proof-reading."

"Please!" she grinned. "That took me twenty-five minutes!"

"Are you suggesting I was underestimating your office skills?"

"Just a little! I'm a teacher. We're our own executive secretaries most of the time." The printer gave a final hum then lapsed into silence, and she gathered up the sheets in the tray, slipped them into a crisp new manila folder and handed them to Ty.

"So what is this?" he repeated, clearly intrigued by the smile she couldn't keep from her face.

"Take a look," she told him. "It's rough, but it covers the basics. Program content and ideology. Budget items that will need costing. A list of other local businesses who might be interested in helping to sponsor it. A list of local charities, support groups and welfare agencies to liaise and consult with in order to identify the right kids. Dot points about other issues that would need consideration, such as insurance and liability, but I was running out of time by then."

"The free sailing school." He flipped through

the folder, his attention flicking over her headings and lists. She watched him and waited, until he looked up after two or three minutes. "Sierra, this is great. This is fabulous. You did this in, what, two hours?"

"Just about."

"And you worked on it because…?"

"Because it's always been a great idea. You're in a position to do it, you want to do it, and you should. And my principal was right. The special needs science program looks great on my resume. I learned a lot, putting it together, so why not make use of those skills in a different area?"

"Since you had a spare couple of hours."

"Since I had a spare couple of hours. Since it was an idea we shared."

"Wow." He flapped the file against the palm of his hand. "Don't know what to say."

"You don't have to say anything right now. It would be a lot of work to set up the program. You may decide against taking it any further. But…you know…don't throw away that file just yet. I, um, enjoyed doing it."

"I won't throw it away." His voice sounded a little husky, suddenly. "Thanks. I'll put it right on my desk."

* * *

They got home to his place at seven, after a side trip to the store, and brought deli salads, fresh crusty bread and a bottle of red wine into the kitchen. Ty raided the freezer for steaks, poured glasses of wine and switched on the gas barbecue on the deck, while Sierra sliced onions to fry. She had tears streaming down her face from the fumes when the phone rang.

"Hi, Sierra…"

Angie's voice.

No surprise, there.

"I've been calling and calling but you haven't picked up all day," Angie said. "Your cell kept telling me it was switched off or out of range and I didn't want to leave strings of messages."

"How're things? What's up?" Sierra asked, making her questions sound upbeat in the hope that the answers would be, also.

The strategy didn't work.

"Well, he called but he sounded so weird, Sierra."

"Did you ask him about it?"

"Yes, and he got mad and said he didn't sound weird, I was the weird one and just to lay off, because he couldn't stand that I was so paranoid. And, like, am I a paranoid person, Sierra?"

"Well, normally, no, I wouldn't have said—"

"Exactly! You're so right, you see! I'm not. So this isn't me, it's him, and now I'm not sure whether to go up to Columbus and confront him or just play it cool, so that he can't put this on me and if there is something wrong he'll have to be the one to trigger the confrontation. Or should I, like, call him at six in the morning and see who answers—if it's a female voice—or go up and not tell him I'm coming and sit outside his house and—?"

"Okay, sis, now you're sounding paranoid," Sierra said gently.

The open door out to the deck darkened and she saw Ty looking at her across the room. He frowned and looked startled—really concerned, actually, and she didn't understand why until he put his finger to his cheek and made a questioning gesture.

Tears? Crying?

She shook her head, smiled and mouthed, "Onions," and he nodded and laughed, and it was the kind of small, nice moment that they'd had a few other times today.

It reminded her of everything she'd lost when he left Ohio eight years ago, and she recovered her patience with her sister. Todd would hurt

Angie if he dumped her. They'd been going out together for eight months, which wasn't the same thing as being married for four years, true, but Sierra knew that the heart didn't tally dates and legalities when it was breaking.

"So when are you coming home?" Angie asked.

"Coming home? Um, I'm not sure yet, be-cause—"

Ty was still watching and listening. He stepped closer. "Tell her you're not."

"Just a second, Angie." She put her hand over the phone. "Sorry?"

"Just tell her you're not coming home." His words seemed intense and his whole body looked wound tight, all of a sudden.

"But that's not—"

He took a couple more impatient paces.

"Does it matter if it isn't true?" he demanded. "How about if it was true? She's almost twenty-three years old, Sierra. No-one's asking you not to care about her, and not to stay emotionally close, but—never mind if it's good for you—is it good for her to know that you'll come running to kiss everything better the moment she calls with a problem or a need?"

"I—"

"I don't think it is good for her, or for Lena and Jordy, or for your dad. Let them think for a couple of days that you need a vacation—which you do—and that you're going to be here for the next six weeks. Just try it, because I want to see the effect it has, even if you don't."

Sierra carefully took her hand off the mouth-piece of the phone and shifted in the chair. "Angie? At this stage, I'm thinking—"

"You have to let me know, Sierra," Angie cut in, wailing. "You can't keep it open-ended. It's not fair of you to do that, when it affects my plans."

"Which plans does it affect, honey?"

"Well, you know, Dad and... Grocery shopping, and stuff. You know. And we miss you. And getting up to Columbus to see Todd."

"You can't go to Columbus to see Todd if I'm not in Ohio?"

"Oh, come on, you know what I mean. Dad and..."

Ty was still watching her. Sierra knew he was still watching her, even though she'd turned her back on him and even though he was quite silent and still, just inside the doorway. In her imagi-nation he filled the whole space like a looming threat. The back of her neck tingled, and she hated this too-familiar feeling of being stuck in between her husband's blunt attitude toward her family and the demands of her siblings which—which sometimes—

"No, Angie," she heard herself say. "I'm not committing myself to a day or a date right now."

She took in another breath, ready to talk about needing a break, about her tough class this past year, about really appreciating the solitude and the sea, and about Ty actually asking for her help.

But then she didn't say any of it, and there was an almost dizzying sense of satisfaction in just laying out her decision and letting her family deal with it, rather than explaining everything and cajoling them into telling her that of course it was okay, and of course they understood how she felt.

"Sierra!" Angie squeaked, indignant and upset.

"You'll just have to accept that I'm staying longer."

She said a firm good-bye and put down the phone then stood up, stretched her shoulders and turned to meet the look, with his eyebrows raised, that she knew Ty would throw at her.

Yep, there it was, eyebrows and everything.

He started a slow clap at the same time, and that was too much.

"Stop," she told him. "There's no need for you to celebrate this as a personal victory."

He shrugged. "Okay, I'll leave the celebration to you."

"Did it ever occur to you that it might be hard for me to watch them grow up and grow away from me, after I've been almost a mother to them for sixteen years?"

"Did it ever occur to you that eventually they're going to turn you into one of those spinster aunts in big Victorian families a hundred and fifty years ago, who never got to have her own life because everyone, including herself, just assumed she'd go on looking after ageing relatives and baby-sitting nieces and nephews and knitting shawls and socks until she dropped in her tracks?"

"That's not how I see myself."

"That's how they could end up seeing you. Oh, Sierra will do it, she won't mind."

"No, that's not how it is." She shook her head.

He moved closer and kept speaking, merciless about it. "Oh, we don't have to worry about who's feeding the dog while we're away, or watering the plants, or collecting the mail. Sierra will do it. She never takes a vacation. Sierra will babysit. Sierra will take care of Dad. And since she's always available, she can deal with the repair men and run errands to the store and deal with the difficult neighbor." He dropped the mimicking tone. "Never takes a vacation, Sierra, just gets taken for granted."

"Ty…"

He moved closer still, reached out and cradled her forearms in his hands, massaging her skin. "And it gets to me, because at some level if that does happen, no matter how much you love them, you'll be angry and bitter and resentful and it will start to show on your beautiful face, and—"

"Sucking on a lemon?" She pressed her fingertips to her lips.

"Yes. That. See, you can feel it there yourself." He eased her hand away from her face and put his own finger-tips in its place.

Sierra's lips parted, but no protest came out, only a sigh of breath.

Ty continued softly, "I don't want the wind to change sometime in the next few years, and your mouth to get frozen that way." His fingers slid beneath her chin, while the ball of his thumb kept up its feather light caress. "Not a soft, sensual, passionate mouth like yours, Sierra." His hand dropped to her shoulder and he bent close, his words whispering just an inch from her face. "Not a mouth I've gotten so lost in, all the times we've kissed."

Their lips met the moment he finished speaking.

Sierra closed her eyes, swept away in seconds, like a piece of driftwood swept away at high tide. Her body belonged to Ty's in a way she couldn't imagine it belonging to any other man's. She cupped his face in her hands, staking her claim on every inch of his skin, loving the slightly roughened texture of his jaw and the feel of his neck, like tightly braided rope covered in warm satin.

He dipped his head lower and tightened his arms around her, cramping her breath, and she felt a surge of emotion at the knowledge that he was as overwhelmed by this as she was. His physical strength didn't give him any protection at all against the demands of his senses.

For minutes, they couldn't seem to stop, although Sierra distantly knew that they had to. *She* had to, if he wouldn't. But it was so good. His taste and his touch and the way he was as lost in this as she was. Her whole body throbbed and grew heavy. She could have melted on the floor. Finally, however, she summoned some strength and focus.

She dragged her mouth away from his kiss and buried her face in the curve between his neck and shoulder, needing some breathing space so she could attempt to understand the tangled strands in her own feelings. How could she want and need him like this when the marriage they'd both believed in had so badly failed?

Ty didn't try to kiss her again, just held her so that she could turn her head a little to pillow it against his chest, where she felt the hard pull and push of his breathing and heard the thud of his heart.

They both stood very still.

"I don't want love to make me bitter," she said finally. "Not any kind of love. You're right. Love shouldn't do that. But I'm afraid about where this is taking us, Ty. And I think that you have far more power to fill me with regrets than my family does."

He said nothing for almost a minute, and her ears seemed to ring with the silence. "I don't have an answer for that," she heard from him at last. "I don't know what I can tell you. How can I promise that you won't regret the time you're spending here, or the new things we're finding out?"

"You can't," she agreed.

"So what do we do?"

"Now? What do we do right now? Oh, Ty! I

think we just…" She pulled back and spread her hands. "…barbecue."

He hissed the breath out between his teeth. "Yeah, you're right, I guess we do."

While casual on the surface, with Ty in bare feet and faded jeans, the undercurrents as they prepared and ate their meal were anything but. They were both poised on the brink, aware and wanting. He wouldn't let her near the gas grill so she sat in one of the Adirondack chairs, angled so they could talk and she could watch the sea at the same time. In truth she didn't watch the sea very much because it couldn't begin to compete with her view of Ty.

When he stretched over the grill to turn the steaks, the fabric of his jeans and white T-shirt tightened all across the back. Sizzling oil dripped onto the gas flames and they flared up at one point, making him rear back and put the back of his hand across his eyes. Sierra almost jumped up to check that he was okay, but he must have seen her movement, because he waved her back.

"It's fine. The smoke stung a little, that's all." It was still snaking and billowing around him and he stood there with his eyes closed waiting for it to dissipate. Since he couldn't see what she was doing, Sierra stared shamelessly, learning exactly the way every muscle in his body curved, learning the angles in every limb as if she'd have to pass an exam on the subject when she got back to Ohio.

Oh, but she didn't want to think about Ohio, because Ty wouldn't be there.

"I think they're about done," he said a few minutes later.

"I should have brought everything out ready."

"We'll both do it, and it won't take long."

They shuttled to and fro with salads and ketchup and plates and silverware. Ty put on some music and lit a dozen citronella candles to keep the mosquitoes at bay. He set them on the deck railing and the table, where they flickered in the mild evening breeze. The golden light they gave off was magical, and the air smelled of lemon and ocean and barbecue.

From above, Sierra's imagined TV news helicopter crew would only have seen two people eating a casual meal, but from close up so much more was happening. Their eyes kept meeting across the table. Who knew that just one simple, shared gaze could smoke so strongly and tangle so thickly and communicate such depth and such desire?

Ty stretched out his legs so that the fabric of his jeans brushed against Sierra's bare calves and she didn't try to move away. Instead, she took his hand and felt the answering pressure he gave. He brushed his thumb across her knuckles, his touch as gentle as his mouth would have been. Every time he put his glass to his lips she remembered the taste of his kiss, and she knew he could see the memory glowing in her eyes.

They pretended to talk.

Well, no, they really did talk, but for most of the meal they only pretended that what they said was important.

"Steak came out good."

"So tender! And this isn't regular ketchup, is it? It's delicious."

"It's from that little gourmet food store across the street from the entrance to the waterfront. Nickie Allen makes most of the sauces and preserves she sells, and I love this one. She supplies *Nautilus* with some of her lines, but she won't give us her recipes."

"She has the right strategy. Much more profitable to sell you the finished product."

"You have a point!"

They talked about Sierra's ideas for the new

sailing program and Ty muttered something about getting a pen and paper to write down what they said.

"Don't," Sierra told him, as she finished her steak. She didn't want to break the connection she could feel in the air. "We'll remember, won't we?"

The word "we" gave away too much about how she enjoyed sharing his latest plans and ambitions, but he didn't seem to notice.

"I guess we will. If we go ahead with this, though, I want to make sure we've covered everything."

"You'll really think about it, won't you?" she realized aloud. "You'll put in all the groundwork, you won't make a commitment on impulse."

"That shouldn't surprise you, should it?"

"No, and it doesn't. I guess you've always put in the groundwork."

"I've had to. I've always known there was nothing to fall back on but the foundations I'd made for myself. No-one to pick up the slack, cover any debts, bail me out of trouble."

Well, he'd had her to do some of that, for a while, Sierra thought.

For more than four years, in fact.

She would have happily met any need he expressed.

She didn't say it aloud, and as they sipped the last of their wine in silence for a few minutes, she thought about it. Ty obviously didn't agree. He'd obviously never considered her as someone he could fall back on or count on in that way. And apparently he had no idea that she would mind about that, that she might be hurt by it, that being needed and counted on was as important to her as being loved.

No, correction, it was an integral *part* of being loved. It was an integral ingredient in trust. You had to trust the people whom you needed in your life.

Her heart twisted painfully.

Ty had loved her but he'd never needed her, which meant that at some fundamental, unconscious level he hadn't trusted her, so she'd let him go.

Eight years later, the only sign that he might have changed had come in the form of those four short words he'd spoken three and a half days ago. "I'm asking for help." Those words had been enough to make her commit to staying for a few days, even a couple of weeks. Were they enough to let her follow her heart tonight?

She knew where it wanted to lead her, and she knew where Ty himself wanted to go.

Every nerve in her body clamored for it—for him, his body, his love-making.

"Thinking?" he asked softly. "It looks too much like hard work for you, right now."

"It's—um…" She couldn't find an answer. He'd stretched his hand across the table again, and this time he wasn't letting go after one brief caress.

"Not your family, I hope." His fingers tangled with hers and made patterns of delicate sensation on the fine inner skin of her wrist, arrowing awareness straight to her core. There were other places he could touch her like this, moistening, swelling places, where her response would be even stronger.

"No, not them," she managed to say.

"Good. Shall I tell you what I hope you're thinking about?"

"No. Uh…don't."

"Guess it's pretty obvious, huh?"

Yes.

"Uh…" she repeated helplessly.

But he wasn't going to let her get away with that non-answer.

"It's obvious, Sierra," he said. Her gaze was totally trapped in his, now. "And it's obvious what you want to do about it, too, so let's not pretend.

That's one thing I can say about our marriage. One thing I'm proud of, still. We never pretended or lied to each other, and I won't start now. I want you. In my bed. Now, and all night long. And you want it, too."

He sat up and leaned closer. Their forearms pressed together, echoing the press of two whole bodies. He took her other hand, as well, and now his face was only six inches from hers. "You want it," he repeated. "And you know that's only the beginning."

"Beginnings are easy."

"Beginnings are necessary."

"What comes next?"

"How can we know that, before we've taken the first step? I'm not saying it's risk free."

"But you're saying there's no gain without the risk?"

"Yes. Can you argue that? If you're going to, then I need you to argue it now, Sierra, not in ten minutes or half an hour, when we're lying together skin to skin. By then, it will be too late."

Argue it now? How could she argue anything now, when his eyes shone into hers like that, so hot and hungry? When her own body was such a traitor to caution and good sense? When eight years ago suddenly felt like yesterday, and, heaven help her, she was still his wife?

"Ty. Oh, Ty," she breathed. "If I should argue… I've forgotten why. And if you know why, you're not going to remind me, are you?"

"Have I ever struck you as that much of a saint?" he growled.

"No. You're all man. The man I want." She hardly knew what she was saying.

She closed her eyes, felt his breath on her cheek and then his lips brushing her mouth, teasing her, cajoling, letting her know just how much more she wanted, and how much she was ready to give. She kissed him back, pressing her parted lips on his over and over, tasting him and giving him entry, losing all sense of time.

And she knew that even if she somehow managed to call a halt to this now, it would be too late. She'd already given herself to him. She'd given him her heart with every touch of her mouth.

"Come on," he said roughly. "This isn't enough. I can't hold you."

He slid sideways on the bench seat, stood and reached for her, pulling her up in one swift, impatient movement. He ran his hands down her back, cupped her rear and brought her against his hardness, as if to leave her in no doubt. She softened and swelled and ached, her breasts tingling with heat and heaviness, the strength of sensation swamping the slight sting of her sunburn until it faded away.

The French doors that led from the far end of the deck to his bedroom were open, their semi-sheer drapes filling like sails in the evening breeze. Brushing them aside, he led her through, closing only the sliding screens so that it felt as if they were about to make love in the open night air.

The spacious room was in darkness, but light spilled in from the corridor, from the risen moon and from the candles still leaping in their jars out on the deck. Plenty of light to see by. Sierra wanted to see. Impatient, she slid her hands beneath his T-shirt and dragged it upward until he took over and pulled the unwanted garment over his head to toss it aside.

Then she touched his chest. Touched and looked, stroking her fingers down from his broad shoulders and across the hard, squared bulge of his pectorals. He had more hair there, now, than he'd had eight years ago, but it still felt the same—silky and rough at the same time. She loved it, because its texture communicated his maleness so strongly, telling her how much his body contrasted with hers.

She loved that. She'd always loved it. Hard, against her softness. Rough, against the satin of her own skin. Angular, against her curves. She wanted him to know just how soft and different she was, and instinctively reached for him, closing her hands over his and pulling them toward her. He cupped her breasts through her clothing, but that wasn't good enough and she heard a sound of protest and dissatisfaction escape from her own throat.

"Shall I?" he whispered.

"Yes, please."

She closed her eyes and felt his hands brush across her body again. His fingers soothed her tender shoulders and dropped to trace a soft line around the scooping neck of her tank top and back up to the straps. He slid them gently from her shoulders, scarcely seeming to make contact. He must have seen the pink, sore tinge on her skin.

He hooked his thumbs inside the neckline and peeled the tank top down, still moving so slowly and gently that she could hardly breathe. When he reached the swelling slopes of her breasts and saw that her bra was part of her top, he made a sound of appreciative discovery that had her smiling and lapping her tongue convulsively against her bottom lip at the same time.

"This is very clever," he muttered. "Halves the work and doubles the reward."

"Don't stop. Admire the architecture…tomorrow." She could hardly get the last word out.

Instinctively, she arched her spine, offering him her fullness—the softness and curves she'd wanted him to see. He touched her peaked, swollen nipples, brushing them with the backs of his hands almost reverently, as if he couldn't believe they were really his.

If she'd had any words left, she would have told him.

They're yours, Ty. All yours, and nobody else's. They always have been.

He held them and lifted their weight, caressing the tender skin until the ache between her thighs was so strong and hot she couldn't think straight. When he buried his face in the deep cleft he'd made, she grabbed his shoulders and hung on for her life. He dragged the tank top lower and it snagged at the waistband of her capri pants, so she managed to shimmy both the pants and the scrunched up tank down her hips and thighs at the same time.

He'd seen her like this before, naked and wanting, and yet it felt so special and new. There was a thread of shyness in her feelings. How much had her body changed? Her hips and breasts were all a little rounder and fuller now. Did he…?

Yes. He liked it that way. He couldn't keep his hands off her. She came home into his arms, aching for the touch of his most intimate skin, still sheathed inside his jeans and briefs. They almost fought each other, because he was trying to hold her while she grabbed at the zipper and fastening that got in her way.

Finally, he helped her, yanking the metal tag down, pushing at the fabric, his black stretchy briefs straining at the front.

Ohh… Yes… This…

Silk and steel. Pressure and give.

She rocked her hips shamelessly against him, hearing his ragged breathing as a reward. He ran his hands between her thighs and must have known at once that her arousal was every bit as powerful as his. He dipped his head and found her nipples, with his mouth, lavishing moist sensation on each in turn until she throbbed all over.

They slid to the bed, not taking the time to remove the cotton comforter. It was cool and soft and puffy beneath their bodies, like another kind of caress. Time slowed as they reached for each other again, and in both of them impatience battled with the pleasure of each moment. They could let this take all night, or they could surge to fulfilment within minutes. It wouldn't matter which.

Lying on their sides, they touched and explored, remembering, rediscovering, making it new. Ty's mouth was everywhere, hungry and intimate, pushing Sierra to the brink and holding her there. He teased her, withdrawing at the last moment so he could take her hand and place it on his hard length. She gripped and stroked him, feeling his mounting need like an electric vibration that was almost a part of her own body.

Just when she thought he might lose control, he snatched her hand away and touched her intimately again, feeling how ready she was, knowing how effortlessly he would slide into her and bring them both to climax.

"Yes," she urged him. "Don't wait, now." He reached for his bedside drawer and somehow managed to sheath himself while she kept touching him, her impatience overflowing like a brimming cup. Oh, oh, please, please. "Ah…yes!"

Yes. This. She'd forgotten.

Oh, but she remembered now. The physical fullness, the unique vulnerability, the precious emotion of containing her own husband deep within her, feeling him push closer then pull back so he could push closer again, over and over.

She clung to him, close to total abandonment, and when he reached between their bodies and touched her she spilled over into bliss and felt him meet her half way as he surged into her. They both came slowly back to earth without needing to speak a word.

The phone in Ty's living-room began to ring three minutes later.

Chapter Nine

"Leave it," Ty growled.

He'd felt Sierra's body stiffen at the first sound. Now, he had to hold her back or she would have raced for the phone as if expecting life or death news. Finally, she slumped beside him in the bed, her hot, naked body delicious against him. He felt a fresh stirring of need that seemed to build with impossible speed. He'd been on the wrong side of thirty for a couple of years, but with Sierra next to him like this he felt as if he was still in his teens.

"I'm sorry. Habit," she said. "At home, I— You're right, though. It's probably not anyone either of us wants to talk to."

But she still hadn't truly relaxed.

The phone kept ringing. After four long, insistent peals, his answer-machine picked up and they both lay there listening to his message, waiting and hoping for a hang-up.

Didn't happen.

"Sierra?" wailed Lena's voice. "If you're there, you have to pick up, okay? Like, now."

"No, you don't," Ty told her, still pinning her to the bed. "This is what answer machines are for."

"But she sounds—" Sierra began.

Ty felt her tense up again and start to slide away, and the fight went out of him. The peace, too, if that wasn't a contradiction. Such blissful, contented peace, only a few moments ago. But now he felt…empty, resigned, and totally unsurprised. He let her go, his hands trailing clumsily across her skin.

"Are you there, Sierra?" Lena repeated, her wail higher and louder. "I really need you to pick up. Angie is a mess. She's just found out Todd's cheating on her and I don't know how to handle it. You have to talk to her. Like, the second you get this message."

Sierra moved like a mother cat, sleek and fast and supple and on the attack. He heard her moments later, "Honey? Is that what's been going on? Oh, poor Angie! Is she there with you? Can I speak to her?"

She must only have gotten to the phone a fraction of a second before Lena would have put it down at her end.

I should have tripped her up, Ty thought, or locked her in.

Held her back by her long, beautiful hair, even.

He felt just about that primitive, right now.

Suppressing the cave man urges, he rolled stiffly out of the bed, like a binge drinker after a hard night. The air had cooled with the effect of the ocean breeze. He climbed into his jeans and grabbed his T-shirt from the floor but didn't put it on. Instead, when he reached Sierra at the phone, sitting hunched in a chair with her bare swollen breasts pressed against her bare, silky knees, he bunched the T-shirt up at the neck and slipped it over her head.

The garment had lost his body heat but it still had his scent and he wanted that. He wanted it surrounding her, reminding her, making its claim on her—if she would take any notice.

Yeah. Right. What chance was there of that?

Feeling the soft cotton around her neck, she

gave him only the tiniest nod of thanks. He didn't
know who was on the other end of the line. Still
Lena? Or was it Angie, by this time?

Didn't matter. She frowned and went, "Uh
huh," and did all her usual caring-listening-giving
stuff. Automatically, she threaded her free arm
through the T-shirt sleeve then swapped the phone
into that hand and pushed her arm through the
second sleeve, shaping her body through the
action with impossible, unconscious grace.

The body of the T-shirt fell down around her,
covering those gorgeous breasts and hips and
reaching as far as her thighs. She pulled it down
to a chaste point half way to her knees, but even
like that she looked so achingly sexy, her long,
smooth legs leading Ty's gaze and his imagi-
nation higher to all the lush secrets that lay
beyond the stretchy white hem.

Ty wanted to snatch the phone out of her hand
and yell down the line.

Deal with it, Lena. You're a grown up, and so
is Angie. Your big sister dealt with grieving for
your mother, taking care of your father and virtually raising you from when she was fourteen.
She loves you to death, and you trade on that all
the time, and it's not fair.

But there was no point in saying it, either in anger or with understanding.

He went back to his room, found a clean shirt and shut himself in his office, not wanting to hear another word of the call.

It took Sierra twenty minutes to get off the phone. She couldn't get the detail she wanted from Lena. Angie was just "a mess" plain and simple, and Sierra had to come home.

Like, now.

Tomorrow at the latest, driving half way through the night if she had to.

"So can I speak to her?" she finally asked.

"If she can talk," Lena said.

"Try her. I want to find out what really happened."

After five minutes of silence and those odd thumpy and echoey sounds you get in the background when someone puts down the phone and goes out of the room, Angie finally picked up. The first thing Sierra heard was a long, shuddery sob.

"Hey…" she said.

"Hey, yourself." Big, ragged sniff.

"Tell me about it."

"Well, I drove up there."

"To Columbus. Did you tell him you were coming?"

"No, because I didn't want to give him a chance to cover his tracks."

"Was that fair? Kind of condemning him without a trial, don't you think?"

"Did you tell Ty you were coming to Stoneport?"

Two points to Angie.

"That was different. I wasn't planning to accuse him of anything, I was just—"

Asking for a divorce.

Am I still doing that?

"Okay, it's not relevant, anyhow," Angie cut in on Sierra's significant silence. "I'm sorry, I shouldn't have said it. We're talking about Todd. Who had a woman in his apartment when I arrived."

"Fixing the plumbing, possibly? Having a meeting? His cousin?"

"Oh, come on, Sierra! I knew!"

"Honey, did you ask?"

"Okay, one, I heard giggling before I even rang the bell. Two, there was no-one else in the apartment. Three, he looked as guilty as…as, oh, a dog who's just chewed your best shoes. Four, she left without speaking to me, beyond one little, tiny, triumphant, insincere hi."

"And what did he say?"

"That he didn't know what my problem was, lately. And I said I'm not the one with the problem. And he said fine, neither was he, so obviously our feelings were mutual and we'd both be better off not seeing each other any more."

Which was where the relationship stood right now, apparently, although Angie took another ten minutes to definitively outline this fact, and of course she didn't feel better off not seeing Todd. She was sobbing again by the end of the story, peeling another layer of skin off Sierra's tortured heart with every hiccupping, shuddering sound.

And whether Todd really had cheated on Angie, or whether her insecurity had driven him away, the bottom line stayed the same. He'd dumped her and she was hurting and she wanted her sister.

Big question—would her sister go?

"I'll call you in the morning, okay, Angie?" Sierra told her. "Let's sleep on it and see how everything looks then."

"How is it going to look any different?" Angie answered, and it took another few minutes of listening and soothing before Sierra could put down the phone.

Once she had, she curled her legs up higher on the chair and wrapped her arms around them, releasing the scent of Ty's T-shirt into the air around her. It smelled of laundry soap and some sweet, nutty kind of anti-perspirant, with faint afternotes of barbecue smoke and ocean breeze. It felt soft, like Ty's arms, and it was enough to keep her warm, the way his body would have done.

It made her think of him, but it wasn't him, and she wished it was.

He'd disappeared into his office and the door stood firmly closed. Light seeped from underneath it, along with the faint sound of computer keys clicking occasionally. He might as well have hung a Do Not Disturb sign on the door.

Sierra wasn't stupid, and she knew him pretty well. He'd heard Lena's voice and a part of her own end of the conversation with Angie. He knew the decision she had to make, and he was telling her loud and clear, "Make it on your own."

Her stomach felt heavy, and her spirits so torn she could almost hear the sound of ripping. She didn't want to let Angie down, and yet she knew Ty would consider that she was simply repeating the same old pattern. The same old destructive pattern that was going to turn her into a Victorian maiden aunt not too many years from now, according to him.

They'd had a long day and she was tired, her emotions were ragged and her skin burned hotter, chafed in places by the loose neckline of Ty's shirt. She hadn't even noticed her sunburn as she and Ty made love. His hands had been everywhere on her body and she hadn't felt a thing, but now her shoulders and upper chest stung.

Not the best state for making decisions of any kind. Not about going back to Ohio, and not about how she felt now that she'd let herself and Ty renew the deepest intimacy of their marriage.

Leave it till morning, she decided. Go to bed and try to get some sleep.

She made a pit stop in the bathroom at the foot of the stairs and wished she had some soothing, medicated cream to put on her burned skin. Her make-up bag yielded nothing that looked quite right.

The light was still on and those computer keys were still clicking in Ty's office. She could check his own private bathroom without disturbing him, and the momentary doubt she felt about invading that space seemed foolish when she thought of how close they'd been with each other less than an hour ago.

Behind the sliding mirrored door of his bathroom cabinet, she found what she was looking for—a specially formulated after-sun lotion. She took off the cap and was just about to pool some of the cool, lightly scented white liquid in her palm when she felt movement behind her and Ty was there.

"For your sunburn?" he said. "Let me do it."

He took the tube of lotion from her hand before she had a chance to protest and she closed her eyes, berating herself for letting him take control. She heard the squirt of the liquid onto his fingers, then felt him close behind her as he gently lifted the neckline of the T-shirt. At the first touch of the cold lotion she shivered, but then its cool wetness began to soothe and temper the burn.

Ty's touch was so soft, so much like a caress as he painted the lotion across her collarbone and out to the knobs of her shoulders. Deliberately like a caress. He wanted to remind her of what they'd shared less than an hour ago—as if she needed that! She felt his breath on her neck and the strength of his body just inches from her back, and had to fight not to sigh back against him. It would feel so good to do that, and then to turn into his arms.

At any moment, she expected his mouth to brush the nape of her neck, and inwardly she was already quivering at the thought. Maybe she wouldn't turn into his arms. Maybe she'd stay like this, feel his lotion-scented fingers slipping around her neck, dropping to her hips, finding the entry offered by the loose hem of his T-shirt and sliding up again, across her stomach to her breasts…

"So, are you heading back tomorrow?" His matter-of-fact tone caught her by surprise.

Her eyes snapped open, confronting their twin reflections in the mirror, and she realized he must have seen in it exactly how close she had come to a complete surrender. Clearly, however, he wasn't planning to help her out by providing too much of a pull in that direction. She was on her own.

"I'm not going to decide until the morning," she answered.

"No? I half expected you to find you packing your bags ready to leave town tonight."

"Credit me with some common sense, Ty." She spoke shortly, trying to snatch back a small amount of pride, after betraying herself to him so completely. "It's a twelve hour drive. I'm not going to sit at the wheel all night."

"But if you do go, you'll do it in one day?"

"I took two, coming down, but... I'm not sure. I'd check into a motel if I felt I was getting too tired."

"There." He stepped back, capped the lotion and reached to put it back in the cabinet. "How's that feel now? Better?"

"Much, thanks."

If I can manage to ignore the frustration in every other part of my body, that is.

"Hang on to the T-shirt," he said. "Sleep in it, if you want, since it already has lotion all around the neck."

"Um, yes, okay. That makes sense." She'd worn the pretty cotton nightgown she brought with her, each of the three nights she'd spent at his house, but, yes, there was no point in getting lotion all over it tonight.

"I'm planning to head into town at around six-thirty, tomorrow," Ty said, "so I can wake you as early as six if you want to get a good start."

"That clock in my room has an alarm, doesn't it? I don't need you to wake me."

"Whatever works for you. See you in the morning." He paused, then shrugged. "Or not."

"Ty, I'm not just going to sneak out without letting you know!"

"And I'm just letting *you* know that it's your decision. No pressure."

"But plenty of unstated opinion."

"My opinion doesn't have to count. *Doesn't* count, in fact, does it? On this issue, it never has."

"That's not—!"

Fair?

True?

But he'd already left. So even if she'd chosen a final word, and had spoken it to his retreating back as he strode along the corridor, she would have had to almost yell it in order for him to hear.

She slept the night wrapped in his T-shirt, with the smell of the after-sun lotion adding to the mix of evocative scents, reminding her of their day on the water and the cool touch of his fingers on her skin. She didn't sleep well, and woke at six with no clear decision made.

Ty heard Sierra moving around upstairs when he was already in the kitchen, brewing coffee and flipping eggs and bacon on a griddle, at ten after six. Since she was up this early, he drew the obvious conclusion—she was going back—and he was…kind of astonished, actually…at how much it ripped at his gut, when he'd been expecting exactly this, which meant he should have been prepared.

Damn his sense of honor and pride, last night!

He could have seduced her with that sweet-smelling lotion, he knew it. He'd started to. He'd seen the effect his touch had had. And he should have done it. Damn fairness and principles and this stubborn belief of his that if he railroaded her or blackmailed her or confused her into choosing him over her family, then the victory wouldn't mean anything.

He should have done it anyhow, because he didn't want to lose her.

Not again.

Not when he knew down to the numbness in his fingertips and the lump of lead in his stomach just how much it had hurt last time, and that it wouldn't be any different the second time around.

In fact, it would probably be worse.

He added another egg and a couple more slices of bacon to the griddle, more bread to the toaster, and when she appeared he told her, "I made you some breakfast. No need to drive on an empty stomach."

"I haven't decided yet if I'm going…"

"Okay, then," he said evenly, as if the sudden

wash of complicated, breath-bated relief in his body hadn't happened. "In that case, no need to make a decision on an empty stomach."

"…but thanks, anyhow. I—I appreciate the thought." She hugged her arms around herself, looking a little chilly in her stretch jeans and another little tank top, pink this time, that would leave her still-tender skin free of chafing.

"Are you going to wait until you hear from Angie or Lena again?" he asked, flipping toast onto plates and eggs onto toast. "Is that what's holding up the process?"

"Uh…"

"Talk to me about it, Sierra."

"I guess it's about needs," she answered slowly, pausing after that last word. "I'm trying to work out what's best for Angie. If she needs me to go back, or—you said this—if it would be better for her, in the long run, if I stayed here as planned. I mean, my heading home to Ohio isn't going to get Todd back for her. It's just a question of—"

"Needs," he echoed, sliding a plate in front of her, at the kitchen table, and getting out glasses and mugs to pour orange juice and coffee.

"Yes." She looked up at him through her lashes, with this cautious, hopeful, questioning look on her face that he didn't understand, and that maybe she didn't, either. "Some people do have them, Ty."

"You have them," he answered quickly. "And you ignore them, which could be why everyone else ignores them, too."

"I think we've had this conversation."

He sighed. "Yeah. We have."

They ate in a prickly silence that wasn't comfortable.

"I'm going to call Angie," Sierra finally said. "But it's too early now. She won't be up."

"So why are you up?"

"I couldn't get back to sleep. Now, let me clear up, here, because I know you wanted to get into town early."

"Planning on saying good-bye, before I go?"

"Don't say it like that, Ty, as if it's a challenge."

"Well, I guess it is a challenge, so…"

"No," she said shortly. "I'm not planning on saying goodbye."

Ty didn't know if that was good news or bad news, and he sure as hell wasn't going to ask, when the temperature in the room seemed to be dropping by the second, even as the sun climbed higher above the sea. He left the house five minutes later.

Sierra listened to him go and knew she didn't need to wait until she'd talked to Angie before she made her decision. This wasn't about Angie's needs, or even her own. It was about Ty. Just a few minutes ago, she'd thrown him the perfect opportunity to tell her he needed her to stay…*needed* her…wouldn't be whole without her…the way she knew she wasn't totally whole without him. She'd just lobbed it up for him, like lobbing a soft, squishy ball for a two year old child to catch.

Apparently, he hadn't even seen it bouncing away.

She went up to her room to pack, and there was his T-shirt still draped across the bed, where she'd left it after her quick shower. She reached for it, picked it up, buried her face in it and it was almost like burying her face against Ty's body. It still smelled like him, and like her, and like the lotion—like their whole history together, in one long inward breath.

Sierra felt this horrible, gut-weakening temptation to lay it in her suitcase on top of the rest of her clothes and take it home with her so she could—oh, Lord!—*sleep* with it, or something.

No.

Don't do this to yourself. Pick it up and put it in the laundry hamper for him instead.

There. That's right. Good girl.

She packed her things in the car, left Ty a note which took her a long time to write even though it didn't say very much, and tried calling home because it was eight o'clock, now. No-one picked up.

She didn't leave a message, even though it would have been easy enough just to say, "I'm on my way." And she didn't try Angie's cell phone, in case that ended up with Angie standing with it pressed to her ear and sobbing in the middle of the supermarket or the mall, so that half of Landerville would know by lunchtime that Todd had dumped her.

Instead, she simply made sure that Ty's house was closed up properly, got in her car and started to drive. She could stop somewhere along the road and call home again later, when she was ready for a break.

How long would that take, she wondered. There was a sour emotion welling high in her chest that she couldn't name, and her face—particularly her mouth—already felt tense and tired.

Chapter Ten

So.

Had Sierra gone back to Ohio, or hadn't she?

The question colored the first two hours of Ty's day in such a distracting way that he couldn't concentrate and completely wasted his early morning start in the little office at the marina. At eight-thirty he gave up and called home, hanging on his hope of hearing her pick up at the other end of the line.

She didn't.

He got his own recorded message on the machine, and drew the obvious conclusion. Still, he said her name—"Sierra?"—then waited an embarrassingly long time—he would probably be able to hear his heavy breathing, later, if he played back the machine—just in case she might grab the phone after all.

Shoot!

Why was he doing this to himself? Hadn't he learned long ago that it wasn't safe to count on anyone but himself?

Yeah, all very nice in theory.

When Sierra had come into his life over thirteen years ago, she'd blown that idea right out of the water within a few months of their meeting. His only pathetic hope had always been that if he didn't admit to how much he ached for her, how much *more* he felt himself to be when they were together than when they were apart, then it might pass unnoticed by anyone, leaving him safe.

Confrontation time. He couldn't pretend to himself any more. He'd noticed. He wasn't safe. He was as naked and vulnerable as a newborn baby. And he wouldn't have pretended to Sierra about any of this, any more, if she'd been here.

Only she wasn't.

She'd gone.

Back to square one, for both of them.

He was so angry and so powerless to do

anything about it, he felt as if his insides had turned to glass. Bachelor of the Year, huh? Hell, if only it was true! If only he'd pushed through their divorce years ago, so that she never would have needed to show up here! If he hadn't been so pig-headed and stubborn about it, he could have spared himself this second raging fever of loss and pain and failure.

Working purely on automatic pilot with his brain fuzzy and throbbing, he barely registered the burring sound of the phone on his desk and only snatched it up after several rings. It was Cookie, who never phoned through from the front desk to his private office. She usually just yelled. Now, she told him in a cooing, executive secretary voice that was nothing like her real one, "I have Lucy Little from *A-list* magazine here at the front desk to see you, Mr. Garrett. Are you available?"

Sighing between gritted teeth, he answered, "Sure, show her in," because his current emotional state didn't seem like a good enough reason for saying no.

Lucy was here to say good-bye, it turned out, and her brittle manner stressed too hard that flirting wasn't on her agenda. It seemed like way more than four days since she'd shown up at *Tides* to let him know she was back in town.

"I'm sorry if we've misread each other's signals a couple of times," she told him, perched stiffly in the chair across from his cluttered desk.

Ty didn't think he'd misread any of hers, but didn't trouble to say so. "Will there be a second article?" he asked.

"On further consideration, no, there won't," she said. "My editor doesn't feel that there's been enough sustained interest in the story. I'm sorry if that's a disappointment."

He laughed. "Trust me, it's not! I'm not hungry for my fifteen minutes of fame."

"No. Okay."

"But thanks for all the work you've put in, and for the—uh—effort you made to bring the issue of boating safety to public attention."

"You're welcome." She stood, as polite as an etiquette book, just the way he had been. "Please give my best regards to your wife."

And that was it.

Ty was done with being the Bachelor of the Year.

Now he just had to get himself organized on the Divorce of the Century. Which ought not to be too hard for a man who'd built a company like

Garrett Marine almost from scratch in just eight years, right?

He heard Cookie pouring water into the coffee maker, and came out of his private office to order the biggest mug in their collection. Then he told her, "I'm going to make a complete inventory of the sailing equipment today, Cookie," as if this was an incredibly hard-headed and brilliant corporate decision on his part, and one which, if he floated his company on the stock market, would rocket its shares skyward in the first hour.

Cookie had just finished giving him a very confused, are-you-sure-you're-feeling-quite-well-today-boss look when the nautical bell jangled beside the front door and Sierra walked in.

Ty's head felt as if it was going to explode.

"What are you trying to do to me?" he yelled at her. "I called home and you obviously weren't there. I thought you'd left for Ohio. I thought it was over. Again. I thought—"

"That I'd left. Yes, I had."

"Unh!" He didn't like being right on the issue. It felt like a punch in the gut.

"But then I came back," Sierra told her husband simply.

She met Ty's flaming stare full on, with a

flaming stare of her own. He looked angry, but there was something else in his eyes, also—the same bleak, frozen pain that she felt herself. How could their feelings for each other possibly be this complicated?

"I turned around just before the Interstate," she said. "I needed to say goodbye to you face to face…and I was too angry to drive."

"*You* were too angry!"

Cookie chose that moment to slip past them, pausing for the shortest possible time on the way.

"Errands," she muttered. "Back later, okay?" Then she gabbled, "Ty, don't forget that *Moderation* got back from her charter to Bermuda last night, and she's all cleaned and tied down at her mooring, keys and alarm fob in the safe, if you, like, need, oh, somewhere to, you know, like, in private."

"Right," Ty said.

Cookie disappeared, locking the front door behind her.

Sierra took a shaky breath. She was close to tears, and scared by the power of her own anger. You could only feel this angry toward someone you loved.

"All you had to say this morning was that you needed me, Ty," she said. "I lobbed it up. I practically had it on TV autocue for you. And you didn't say it. You've never said it." Her throat tightened and her voice went strange. "That's why I could never consider that our marriage was just about the two of us. Because never, in our whole marriage have you ever said it, or shown it, or—"

He froze. "Hell, Sierra! Doesn't it go without saying that I need you? Isn't it obvious?"

"No, Ty, it's not. It's not obvious at all. You want me—" She cut off, hugging her arms around her own body as she remembered the surging force of his desire, the way he touched her, and what it did to her.

Oh, but she had to be stronger than this!

"I know you want me," she tried again.

"No," Ty suddenly said. "Okay. Stop. Don't say it now. Hell, yes, I do want you, but if there's— Cookie was right. Let's get out of here. Do this properly. Give our marriage, or our divorce, whichever it is, the space it deserves. Matt and Adam will be here any second."

He strode into his private office, his impatience brimming over like a cup of coffee poured too full. Standing in the doorway, Sierra saw him open the safe and grab a couple of things from inside, before he clicked the combination shut again.

"Let's go," he said, the way he always did.

And she followed.

The way she once hadn't.

He took the back way, and sure enough they both saw Matt and Adam ambling like seasoned sailors on dry land toward the building they'd just left.

"Going to check *Moderation*," Ty called out to them.

"Sure," the sailing instructors called back.

The boat was the biggest in Ty's fleet of charter yachts, and there was no moderation about any inch of it, Sierra saw at once, as she approached the boat in his wake. The high-tech alarm system that warded off thieves or vandals or even just curious tourists wasn't just for show.

The luxury cruising yacht had to be sixty feet long, with room for cabins and bathrooms, living space and a gourmet kitchen. As Cookie had said, the boat was fully tied down right now, all its equipment stowed away and its portholes and windows covered over.

Showing a speed and efficiency that left Sierra breathless, with a spinning head and only a hazy idea of what the sleek yacht actually looked like, Ty had the two of them on board and below deck in less than a minute, and he didn't waste time in getting back to the crunch point in their confrontation, the second they'd gained the privacy he'd been looking for. Now that the hatch-like door leading down from the deck had closed behind them, no-one would know they were on board, even from just feet away on the dock.

"I want you," he repeated. He paced around the huge cabin, coming to a restless halt beside the mahogany bar, where he leaned, his body full of impatient, aggressive angles. "Was that where we got to?"

"Somewhere around that point," she drawled. "Agenda item number two."

He ignored her. "But for some crazy reason you think I don't need you. It can't be because I'm not dependent on you like your Dad with his medication, and your sisters with their boyfriend problems."

"Don't belittle what's happening to Angie, Ty," Sierra cut in. "Don't we both know that this kind of thing really hurts? Aren't we getting a big, fat reminder of that, right now?"

"So it *is* because I'm not dependent on you? Is that what you're saying? It's because I never used to make long, whiny phone calls to you about losing my video store membership card, or forgetting to buy milk?" He swore. "Is that what you wanted from me? You can't be serious."

She spread her hands. "Can't I? Okay. I'm not serious."

"No. That's not what you mean. Let's try and understand this. Talk to me, don't close up." He came toward her and gripped her upper arms, just short of causing pain. She felt his warmth and his strength radiating in her direction like a blast of summer sun. "I want to hear this."

And he looked so fierce and so sincere about it that she had to rekindle her hope, and she had to find a starting point.

"Four days ago," she began carefully, "when we were sitting in your sedan in the alley, you said to me, 'I'm asking for help.'"

"Yeah, sure, I remember." His grip softened a little and he held her more closely, his palms flattened against her back and his blue eyes steady and watchful. The pull between them was so strong it felt like a rogue ocean current, dragging her down.

"And the only reason I decided to stay was because you'd said it," she went on. "Because in the four years of our marriage, and in the time we knew each other before then, you'd never said something like that. *Anything* like that. You'd never given the slightest sign or word that I was important to you in that way. That I was *necessary* to you."

"But, Sierra, of course you were." His voice rasped, and dropped. "You *are*. Didn't the marriage certificate say it loud and clear? Did you really need the words from me?"

She shook her head. "You wanted me, you even loved me, but if you didn't need me, and if you couldn't say that you needed me, then at some level you didn't trust me, and I couldn't have a marriage without those things. Shared need. Shared trust. It wasn't just that you never said any of it, Ty, you never seemed to show it, either. You did what you wanted, and I could follow along if I liked. Take it or leave it."

"Sierra…"

"I guess if I'd thought you had the need and the trust—not that I understood it this clearly at the time, but at some level I knew—then I might have tried harder to find a way through, eight years ago. But without that… Still, even now, without that, I can't. It's just not possible."

"It is possible," he answered. "It has to be possible. You're wrong about all of this. Which has to be my fault as much as yours, I know that.

My fault *more*. But it's not too late for me to say it, Sierra. Is it? Is it too late?"

"Oh, Ty…"

He kissed her hair and her jaw and her neck, and she closed her eyes. She was the one without trust right now, because she didn't trust that they'd really gotten through this with just a few minutes of anger and some hot, honest words, shut away on a luxury boat with the sun shining on the water and the docks outside.

Was this really enough?

"I do trust you," he went on. She felt his breath against her skin and his hands on her body like hot branding irons. "I always have. I've trusted you to understand my need for you without me having to say it."

"Or show it?" Her voice cracked again. "You never showed it, either, Ty."

"Or even show it, I guess. I'm not a man who enjoys feeling vulnerable. Does any man willingly admit to that? But you know about the childhood I had, the independence and self-sufficiency I *had* to have, so early on, or I would barely have survived. I needed you, Sierra. I trusted you. I trusted you with my heart. Is there really anything more you need to hear from me than that?"

He ran his hands down her back and buried his face in the fall of hair that shadowed her neck. Thrills of electric sensation chased each other up and down her body, like fingers chasing on the strings of a harp.

Was there anything more?

Sierra couldn't think straight. Her body throbbed and felt heavy with wanting him. "I—I need to phone Angie."

Every muscle in Ty's body went stiff and still, and she could almost feel the effort it took for him to speak in a neutral tone when he asked her, "To tell her…?"

She opened her eyes and looked him in the face. His eyes glittered with suspicion and…was that desperation she saw? "That I love her," she said steadily. "That she can call me any time she needs to talk, and that I'm staying here. With my husband. With you."

She waited not knowing how he'd react. With sarcasm? For at least twenty slow heartbeats, he didn't say anything at all as the stiff, suspicious angles to his body gradually softened. Finally, he pressed his forehead against hers and whispered, "Thank you."

Hot tears filled her eyes. "You're welcome," she whispered back.

"You don't know how much I...here you go...*needed,* really needed, for you to say that."

"Yes, I do know."

"We'd have lost our last chance if you'd gone back to Ohio today."

"I know."

"Oh, Sierra. Oh, sweetheart..."

Their noses bumped gently as they looked into each other's eyes, and the side of the boat bumped gently against the dock. Their mouths met and melted together, like fudge melting in a pan, slow and silent and indescribably sweet. Sierra had forgotten that Ty could kiss this way—no demands, no impatience, just a heaven of softness, right in this moment.

Their endless kiss was a promise and a vow, binding them together more securely than the marriage certificate they'd both been prepared to throw away just a few days before. They were together again, joined in body and spirit, with all that this meant.

All. A million things.

"Ty, what are we going to—?" Sierra started to say, but he put a finger on her lips, then kissed her again, building the fire inside them both until it was white hot.

"No details," he said. "Just let me make love to you. Please?"

"Oh, yes, please! Oh, I want that so much, to seal this."

"Then nothing's stopping us."

He meant right here, and right now.

She gasped when she realized. "Ty, do you really think—?"

But any half-hearted protest evaporated before she could even form the words, and he grinned back at her. The air between them sizzled and almost seemed to glow. He'd already flicked the straps of her tank top from her shoulders. "I hope you're not going to tell me this isn't private enough?"

"Um… Well…"

"The windows are covered over. There could be people just a few feet away from us on the dock who'd have no idea we were here. Isn't it comfortable enough?"

His hands at her waist dragged the tank top lower, so slowly that she could feel the air on every newly revealed pore of skin. She arched her spine and let her head loll back the way it wanted to, too dizzy to take control.

"Comfortable?" She could hardly breathe. Ty curved his palms more tightly around her then slid upwards, nudging the undersides of her already aching breasts with his thumbs. Her nipples slipped free and he stroked them, making them peak instantly with need. "It's— Yes. Oh, it's perfectly comfortable. That…what you're doing…is very, very comfortable."

"Mmm, I was hoping for that reaction. Come with me."

"Okay." She let him lead her to the long, sage green leather-upholstered bench seating that fitted against the boat's side, facing the bar.

"And, here, is it sufficiently opulent?" he asked. "Can't argue that one, Sierra." His voice was so low and seductive it was a caress more than a sound. "This leather is like velvet. Feel."

He took her by the wrist and guided her fingertips slowly and lightly over the curved and padded seats, the way she wanted him to guide her fingertips down the velvet length of his arousal.

"You are soooo doing this on purpose, aren't you?" she gasped.

"And you soooo don't want me to stop."

"No, you're right. You're right, I don't."

So he didn't.

They fought and laughed and almost sobbed as they took off each other's clothing and flung it aside. The boat rocked with their movements, making Sierra's happy dizziness grow more intense. She would fall off her feet if Ty wasn't holding her. Light seeped into the cabin from the covered portholes, and the air around them was warm from the sun outside.

Ty lay back on the leather and pulled Sierra down to his chest, cradling her loosely and grinning up at her. "Boats are so nice for this. The way they rock, and that little sense of danger. Do you remember?"

"That time one summer when we—?"

"Yes, on the lake, after dark, in the old mirror dinghy, with a couple of quilts and pillows we'd brought, and our skin smelling like insect repellent except for all the places we wanted to kiss." He brushed her mouth with his, teasing her.

"There were too many of those, I remember," she said. "Some of those places got bitten."

"Didn't even notice until afterward, though, did we?" He rolled onto his side and slid down across the velvety leather to nuzzle the soft valley between her breasts.

"No!" She laughed.

"Just didn't seem to matter." His mouth made a line of warm imprints down toward her navel.

"And then we kissed them again," she reminded him, "and they felt better."

"How's your sunburn today," he whispered. "Can I kiss that better?"

"Mmm, yes, please… No, but, Ty, I didn't get sunburned *there*…" She gasped again, and he took no notice of her protests at all.

Chapter Eleven

"Or we have this gorgeous set of matching bracelet, necklace and earrings in rubies and white gold," said the sales assistant in Wilmington's best jewelry store. She lifted the lid on a crimson velvet box to reveal the matched set, lying on a stretch of cream satin.

"That's more like what I'm looking for," Ty said.

"They're beautiful pieces," the sales assistant agreed. She talked about the successful New York jeweller who had made them, where the rubies and gold had come from and how many carats they added up to, then she waited in hushed expectation for Ty's verdict on the quality of what he saw.

But he wasn't thinking about jewellers or ruby mines or carats at all. He was only thinking about Sierra. How the pale, gleaming gold would look against her newly tanned skin. How the glowing rubies would contrast with the darkness in her eyes. What he would say when he gave them to her, and what she might say or do in return.

Print hot kisses on his mouth.

Press her body against him.

Cry and smile at the same time.

All of the above might be nice. He almost felt like crying himself, and he'd already been smiling for hours.

They had made love twice on the boat this morning. First, that frantic explosion of feeling on the soft leather banquette beside the bar. Nowhere near enough. They'd both agreed on that immediately afterward, still breathless, while a tiny beam of reflected light seeping in from somewhere danced crazily on the ceiling as the boat slowly stopped rocking.

They'd taken it more lazily the second time around, slipping into the master cabin, which was as lavishly appointed as a cruise ship's best stateroom, and slowly discovering each other. The little spot just under her ear that made her gasp when he kissed it. The perfect meeting point between pleasure and pain that he found when she raked her nails lightly across his small, furled nipples.

Afterward, Ty had poured lime juice and soda water at the bar and Sierra had explored the whole interior of the luxurious boat. She'd worn his T-shirt again—nothing but his T-shirt, with her long legs stretching below it—and her curiosity and pleasure had given him a breathtaking fantasy that sometime before the end of summer he might steal away with her for a couple of nights of lazy puttering up the coast toward Pamlico Sound in the beautiful boat.

They'd have balmy August evenings of making love in the darkness on the deck. They'd have French chocolate croissants for breakfast, and caviar and champagne as the sun set. He'd never been able to give her any of that kind of thing during their marriage, those gifts or those luxuries, and suddenly he couldn't wait, he had to give her some of them now. Today.

It had been almost noon by the time they were both dressed and ready to leave the secret sanctuary of the boat.

"I'm going back to your place, Ty, and—"

"Back home," he'd corrected her.

She'd smiled, and it had lit up her whole face. "Home."

"I like the sound of that…"

"Oh, so do I! And I'll call Angie when I get there. She needs to know what's going on. Is it okay if I tell her she can fly down here any time she wants?"

"Of course. Lord, Sierra, you don't need to ask about something like that! I know how much you care about what's happening to her right now."

"And I'm assuming you need to get work done this afternoon, so I'll just hang out on the deck."

"You like that deck."

"I love that deck."

"Want to go out tonight? Somewhere real quiet, where we won't get seen."

"Where we *won't* get seen…" She'd smiled again. "You don't know how good that sounds!"

So they'd parted on the dock—somehow, it had taken them several more minutes—and he'd gone up to the main office and underachieved for several hours until he couldn't stand it any longer. At which point the whole thing about caviar and champagne and spoiling her with gifts had totally overtaken him and he'd driven into Wilmington like a man possessed, cell phone switched off so

that no-one could call him back to the marina
with some urgent, trivial request, because he had
to do something about spoiling Sierra before he
showed up at home and saw her tonight.

"I'll take it," he told the sales assistant, who
still had her hands hovering over the beautiful
jewelry. He didn't even blink at the price.

She gave a reverent nod. "Gift-wrapped?"

"Please."

The package looked gorgeous in cream and
gold paper, with a triple bow of gauzy gold fabric
ribbon, but as soon as he left the jewelry store, he
knew it wasn't enough. Sierra needed flowers,
too. Lilies or irises or… He didn't know what was
in season, but the florist helped, and he came
away with a huge bundle of pink roses, green
ferns and purple lavender swathed in gold tissue
and purple ribbon. The lavender smelled as sweet
as soap and the rose petals were as pink and
velvety as Sierra's mouth.

Next, he stopped at a gourmet grocery store for
the caviar and champagne.

He grinned all the way home, and kept unconsciously nudging the Porsche above the speed
limit because he couldn't wait. It was nearly six
now, but the sun was still warm and bright. She'd

probably be on the deck. Possibly sun-bathing without her top. She might be asleep, and she wouldn't hear him or waken until he lay beside her and kissed her, with the scent of the flowers around them and the gift-wrapped rubies and gold ready and waiting.

Who knew he was such a romantic?

And who knew he could be so shameless about it?

His first inkling that something was wrong came when the automatic garage door rose silently up and her car wasn't inside. The kissing-on-the-deck fantasy evaporated, but he reminded himself in a reasonable way that she might have had errands to run.

She might even have gone to surprise him at his office, maybe planning to lure him back to *Moderation,* which would have been a great idea. If she didn't get back soon, he might try a counter-surprise and meet up with her on the boat...

But the house seemed to contain a different kind of silence, this afternoon. He looked in the kitchen and found a coffee mug and a plate set in the shiny metal basket on the sink to rinse. He went along to his bedroom, which suddenly seemed far too tidy. The bed was neatly made, and there were no drops of after-sun lotion on the porcelain basin in his bathroom.

Upstairs, the closet in the guest room was empty, and her suitcase was gone.

His scalp tightened, along with his chest. This was...ridiculous.

Wrong.

Unforgivable.

They'd planned dinner.

Correction, they'd planned a whole life.

Together.

Here. Sierra had called it "home" with a radiant smile on her face.

She had asked if Angie could come down and she'd made it quite clear that she wasn't planning to go running back to her sister in Landerville to kiss everything better. What had she said to Ty over breakfast this morning, even before their crucial confrontation on the boat?

Driving home to Ohio wouldn't bring Todd back to her sister.

And yet clearly she'd gone, even though she had to be in no doubt as to what he'd think about that.

He paced through the house, fists balled and throat screaming, not understanding at all. Finally,

he reached his office. That was where he found the
note, sitting on the desk beside his phone.

"I'm sorry," Sierra had written in a hasty scrawl,
which he could barely read. "I've gone home and
I know what that means. I know it blows everything out of the water again. I'm going to have to
live with that. Not quite sure how I'm going to do
it, right now. But Dad's in the hospital. Spoke to
his doctor. It's a coma, with probable septicemia,
and it's serious. Tried to call but you'd left your
office and your cell phone was off. Better this way,
probably. Better that the illusions didn't last long.
I'm going to try to drive straight through. Sierra."

You couldn't drive and cry, when you had to
drive for twelve straight hours. It wasn't safe.
And when your dad was in the hospital in a
diabetic coma, with complications, you had to
stay safe no matter what, so Sierra drove and her
eyes stayed dry. Aching and sore and dry.

She had no shred of illusion about what she
was driving away from.

Her marriage.

Ty.

They hadn't solved anything, this morning.
They'd only thought they had.

They'd twice made passionate love, cocooned on a luxurious, rocking boat on the strength of it, but all it took was one monumental blip on the radar of her life and everything got stripped back to the bone again. What had he said to her this morning, just before they'd made love?

"We'd have lost our last chance if you'd gone back to Ohio today."

He was still forcing her to choose between him and her family, and she'd have to learn to hate him for that, if she could.

This morning, she'd thought she could make the choice he wanted—the choice she'd wanted, too, in so many ways. It was easier when things were comparatively rosy. Angie would come down to Stoneport to get over her broken heart in a glorious beach setting. Sierra would research teaching jobs in the area, help Ty put together their sailing school for disadvantaged kids, and count on school vacations for seeing her family.

Except that with her Dad in the hospital, the fantasy faded. And as she'd said to Ty in the note she'd written, she knew what she was doing, heading north-west. She was putting another mile between himself and her with every passing minute.

Permanently.

Lena's phone call about Dad had come at around two, and Sierra had left Ty's within half an hour. She had questions about how the collapse could have happened, but didn't waste time on asking them over the phone.

"He told us he was on top of his schedule, but I guess he was wrong," was all Lena had said. "Angie and I haven't been able to keep tabs on him the past couple of days. We've both been way too distracted and upset. Obviously."

That last statement had made Sierra feel guilty. Thinking back on it, she knew Lena had intended exactly this, which made her feel angry, too. Was this really the right time to use emotional weapons like that?

You're right, Ty.

Right about some of it.

When Dad is better again—oh please, dear God—I'm going to make a few serious changes, and I'm going to take a long summer vacation every year.

But it wouldn't be by the ocean, she knew, because that would hurt too much.

Her jaw tightened, and her hands cramped around the wheel. Eight hours to go. It would get dark soon, and she should stop to eat and get some coffee. If she got sleepy, she'd just have to find a safe rest area off the highway, and grab a couple of hours of napping in the back seat. She wasn't going to waste time checking into a motel. As long as she reached southern Ohio by around dawn…

As Sierra had hoped, the sun was just skimming the hills to the east, beneath a layer of broken cloud, when she turned off the highway onto the road that led into town. She debated going home first, but decided to head direct for the hospital.

She knew how hospitals worked, from the time of her mother's illness sixteen years ago. They started early. Even if the staff wouldn't let her see Dad right away, she could ask the nurses some questions, find out if there had been any change—any improvement, please God!—overnight.

Entering the building ten minutes later, she smelled breakfast cooking and heard metal carts rattling and squeaking as housekeeping staff pushed them along polished corridor floors. She asked about Dad's room and floor number at the front desk, then took the elevator two flights up.

At the nurses' station, she got a cautious but not terrible report. "He's out of the coma, but we still have cause for concern. He does have septicemia, which means his temperature is pretty high and he may seem confused."

"You have him on antibiotics?"

"We're trying everything to get the right response, honey. He's very sick, but we're getting a little more confident, now."

"What could have caused this? I've been away for several days. I'm usually the one who keeps closest track of his blood sugar levels."

"His blood sugar levels weren't the whole problem. He had an infection in his foot, and it spread to his whole system. You probably know that diabetics are more subject to wounds that are slow to heal. And the infection threw everything else off track. But would you like to see him? We can talk more later, if you have questions, and his doctor will be around some time this morning."

"I'd love to see him."

Too anxious to get here, she hadn't stopped to buy flowers, but the room was already full of them, a tribute to her father's popularity and high profile as Landerville's mayor. Dad seemed almost lost in the profusion of color and scent, and he looked pale, lying against the white hospital sheets.

She took his hand and whispered, "I'm here, Dad."

His eyes fluttered slowly open. "Sierra…" He smiled a broad, slow smile. Then he went back to sleep.

Sierra sat for some minutes, just holding his hand, so relieved at having gotten here safely, to find him apparently "doing better," although to her this only suggested how bad he must have looked before. After a while, he opened his eyes again.

"How're you doing?" she asked.

He smiled again. "Better. Much. Now you're here. Happy to see you. I'm buying the magazine."

"I'm sorry?"

"The magazine company. No more articles about Ty. He says I don't have to do that."

"Does he?" She frowned, her heart jumping pointlessly into her throat at the mention of her husband.

The nurse she'd talked to a few minutes ago had come into the room. She stepped closer and mouthed, over Dad's head, "Confused. It happens. It's the septicemia. It's okay. They say things that don't make sense. He won't remember, once the antibiotics begin to take effect and bring the infection under control."

Dad had already closed his eyes once more.

Sierra felt so tempted to do the same. Dad's rhythmic breathing and his warm hand in hers made her feel sleepy, and she was exhausted after the drive. Since he was so quiet, and clearly wasn't feeling bright enough to talk—in fact he looked fast asleep, now—it wouldn't hurt to rest for a little while, because Angie or Lena or Jordy would probably be here soon and that would wake her up again. She saw a ribbon of highway playing endlessly across her vision the moment she closed her eyes.

And when she opened them again, unconsciously sensing movement and sound, Ty was there, standing tall and strong and gorgeous and definitely forbidding, beside Dad's table full of flowers.

Which was impossible, unless—

"I took a flight last night," he said.

"To serve me with the divorce papers in person?" Her voice came out hard and strident, because she couldn't let him see how much it hurt to suddenly find him here, when she'd thought she might never see him again.

And as she'd fully expected, he was angry with her. She could see it in his face.

"A divorce. Is that what you want, Sierra?" he asked.

"No, of course it isn't. But I don't have a choice. Or rather, a choice is exactly what I have. It's the only thing I have. You've been forcing it on me all along, and when I heard how ill Dad was, I knew there was only one choice I could make."

"Yeah? And what was that?"

"To come back, even though I knew you'd think that was, oh, everything you've been so critical about. The lemon-lipped Victorian spinster, sacrificing herself for her family. The woman who doesn't have the courage to choose *you* over everything and anything else that might be important to her. You said yesterday morning on the boat that if I'd gone back we would have lost our last chance."

"No, Sierra. You've got it wrong. So wrong."

She ignored him. "I've *wanted* to choose you since I came to you in Stoneport. So much. When we made love. When we laughed together." The words started catching in her throat. "When I remembered everything we had, and saw how much you've built, everything you always wanted, so successfully. And what I could contribute to it, too. But how can I love a man who asks me to sacrifice my family? Didn't you understand that from the note I left you? Why are you here?"

"Because I'm not asking you to sacrifice your family, Sierra."

She just laughed at this.

"I'm not. I've never wanted that. Yes, I didn't want you to come running back here to stitch together Angie's broken heart, the way you've tried to stitch everything else together for them all, over the years. I thought you could give her enough love and care just by listening, and that she should be resilient enough to get through it with the support of everyone else she has around her. Your father, Lena, Jordy, her friends."

"Okay, yes, and you convinced me on that, but—"

"But do you really think I don't understand that your dad's illness is different?" His blue eyes blazed. "That I wouldn't want you to drop everything to get to his side? Shoot, Sierra, of course I do! Of course that's the right way to feel! You didn't even give me a chance to say so."

"I had to leave immediately. I tried to call you, but I couldn't get through, and I wasn't going to wait. I didn't think it would make a difference to how you felt."

"And I got here eight hours before you did, rented a car at the airport, saw your father for a few minutes last night."

"The nurses let you see him, even though he was so ill?"

"I told them the situation, and then, yes, they did."

"The situation."

"That I'm his son-in-law, I've been his son-in-law for twelve years, and I care about him. Sierra, we could have taken the flight together. It took two hours, door to door. How could you have thought for a second that I wouldn't have wanted you to do that?"

He came around the end of the bed toward her, and she stood up, overwhelmed by the intensity she saw in his face. "Oh, Ty… I'm—I'm sorry."

"And I'm sorry, too, if I've seemed that hard-line. You have to understand that I'm not asking you to choose," he repeated. "Please understand that. A big advantage to my success is that North Carolina and Ohio are a lot closer to each other, for us, than they once were. Just a short flight away. Saying no to Angie wasn't about asking you to choose me over her."

"I guess it wasn't."

"You know what it was about."

"Sucking on a lemon." She touched her mouth, and felt its softness, knowing that Ty was watching her finger-tips and her lips. "And never getting a vacation."

"All of that. How could I want the woman I love to get so locked away in her sense of duty to others? Not just away from me, but away from all her own needs. The woman I love, Sierra, for always, and the woman I need. Please don't doubt that any more."

"Oh, Ty…"

He kissed her, sweet and slow, with the promise of so much more to come.

They both sensed movement in the doorway, and turned to find Angie herself standing there. Angie and someone else—someone tall and male and around twenty-four years old.

Todd.

Angie looked a little shame-faced about his presence, and about the fact that his hand was closed tightly around hers. "It was his room-mate's girlfriend," she told Sierra. "I flipped out all for nothing."

"The woman in the apartment?" Sierra said.

"He was right. It was all my problem. You

were right, Todd. I've told you that, what, around a thousand times, now, since yesterday?" Angie leaned into him, smiled hugely, looked up into his eyes and stroked his face, before turning back to Sierra.

"Having me in Landerville and him in Columbus was making me paranoid, Sierra, and the closer it got to my moving up there, the more paranoid I got. He was angry, and he was right to be angry, and he's forgiven me, and he came down last night and we talked, and everything is perfect, now!"

She let go of Todd and came toward Sierra, her arms stretched out in a big hug.

"Ah, Angie," Sierra whispered, holding her.

"And I'm so sorry about how much I put on you! How much we all put on you. Lena and Jordy and I had a huge talk last night after we left Dad. Three in the morning, while Todd was asleep upstairs! We blame ourselves for Dad getting ill like this. Lena wants to apologize for that line she delivered to you on the phone yesterday, suggesting it was your fault for not being here."

"Angie…"

"No, let me say it, don't let us off the hook. It gave us a huge scare, and if his doctor hadn't told us that he was showing signs of turning the corner…" Her voice dried to a husky rasp, and her eyes filled. "I'm not sure how we could ever have forgiven ourselves. I'm still not sure how you can forgive us. Do you, Sierra?"

"Of course I do. I know your hearts are in the right place. We've all gotten into some bad habits with each other, over the years."

"Jordy wants to say it, too. And even Dad, a couple of days ago, before he got sick, said a few things about how much things fell apart when you weren't around, and how that wasn't good for any of us. You, most of all. Major wake-up call. You should go live in Alaska, or something, until we tell you it's safe to come back." She gave a little sideways glance at Ty. "Or maybe not Alaska…"

"North Carolina is looking pretty good, right now," Sierra answered slowly.

"Oh, Sierra! Oh, true?" Angie's face lit up. "Oh, yes, because you look—and Ty looks—and what's he holding out to you? What's he giving you? Ohmigosh!" Her voice rose in a squeal of excitement.

Sierra let her go and whirled around, to meet a huge bunch of scented flowers and an exquisitely wrapped gift.

"The flowers survived the plane flight pretty well," Ty said. "And the gift isn't perishable."

"You brought them with you?" He must have put them down somewhere before she'd opened her eyes and seen him, and they'd been camouflaged by all the other flowers and gifts in Dad's room.

"I came home with them at around six yesterday evening, after I'd goofed off shopping for half the afternoon." He stepped closer. "That was when I found your car and your things gone, and your note in my office, and I felt like my heart had died all over again."

"Go," Angie said, pushing Sierra the final distance toward Ty so that she almost cannoned into the huge bunch of flowers. "I'm sensing you two still have stuff to talk about. I'll take care of Dad, if he wakes up, and I'll write down everything the doctor says, if you miss him."

"Thanks, Angie," Ty told her.

Sierra didn't argue with either of them. She took the lavish bunch of flowers from Ty and walked out of the front entrance with them still in her arms a minute later. She was definitely going against the regular flow of traffic that way. People didn't usually walk *out* of a hospital carrying flowers…unless maybe they had a baby in their arms as well.

Ty caught her smiling, and she explained as they walked to her car.

"They'll think it's one of the perks of being the mayor's daughter," he said, as he dropped his arm around her shoulders and pulled her close. "Getting a cut of the flowers."

She leaned her head against his chest, her heart almost ready to burst. "Except that I'm far more interested in the perks of being Ty Garrett's wife. May I see what's in the box? May I guess that it's for me?"

He kissed her hair and the corner of her mouth. "You may see what's in the box, but I think it's really for me." They reached her car and he stopped and held it out to her, standing next to her by the driver's side door.

She laughed as she took it, and handed him the flowers to hold. "Oh, it is?"

"I never did this for you when we were together the first time around," he said, watching her fingers at work on the ribbons and bows. The early sunshine made long shadows around them and dazzling points of light on the chrome and window glass of the cars.

"No, I guess not."

He leaned closer and brushed his forehead against hers. "I was so intent on saving for our future, I think the most glamorous, luxurious gift I ever got you was a rainproof jacket. And the one time I bought you something from the plant kingdom, it wasn't long-stemmed roses, it was a plastic flat full of tomato and basil seedlings for that piece of ground at my grandparents' where you tried to make a vegetable garden."

"Oh, I remember that!" She laughed. "I didn't mind, Ty. I understood."

"Too easily." He kissed her again—her ear, her neck, her jaw, her mouth. "From now on, I'm spoiling you with or without your understanding."

"Then I'm helpless, I guess."

Smiling, she gave him the ribbons and the paper, then lifted the velvet-covered lid of the box. Her eyes went wide and her mouth dropped open. She started to laugh with happiness, and the cream and crimson and gold of the satin and the jewels blurred as her eyes filled with tears.

"Helpless," she repeated, her voice husky. Reaching up to bring his mouth down to hers once more, she added, "And totally in love with my husband."

"Who is totally in love with his wife," Ty whispered, his words mingled in their kiss. "Yes, this is definitely a gift for me, more than for you, sweetheart. To see your face. To know I can make you this happy. To know that this time we've understood what went wrong, and we've got it right now, and to have such faith that we'll never get it so horribly wrong again. I love you so much."

"So much," she echoed, and the roses were slowly crushed between them as their bodies clung closer.

Two months later, Ty reflected on his complicated feelings regarding hospital parking lots as he screeched the Porsche into a vacant spot and checked his watch again. He'd made a blissful new start to his marriage in a hospital parking lot—the memory was still vivid and wonderful—and he'd revisited the scene numerous times over the following few days, making visits with Sierra to her father.

Today though, he was running a little late, and he'd have to apologize to both of them for that…as soon as he could find where he was supposed to be. This wasn't a large hospital—about the same size as the one in Landerville—but certain events could make a man quite a lot less organized and in control than he was accustomed to being.

He finally calmed down enough to read the big directory on the wall in the lobby, headed for the right elevator, got out at the right floor, went along the right corridor, and found both Sierra and her father, reading magazines in the waiting area.

"I'm sorry," he said.

"It's fine." Sierra smiled. "We haven't been called in, yet. I told Dad I really didn't need him to drive me here, but—"

"How many times over the years have you come with me to my doctors' appointments, back home, Sierra?" Mayor Taylor cut in.

He was looking so much better than he had in the hospital in Landerville two months ago. He'd been taking full responsibility for his own health since the huge scare they'd all had then, and his two-week vacation here in Stoneport had put fresh color into his cheeks. Sierra was the one who looked pale and ill, today.

"Seems like the least I could do," Mayor Taylor continued, "since you're running to the bathroom every half hour and we even had to bring chilled water and a box of dry crackers for you in the car."

"I'm fine," Sierra insisted again.

"I'm with your Dad on this one," Ty told her.

His heart flipped when he looked at his wife. Eight weeks pregnant. When you'd been married for twelve years and decided it was time to start a family, you didn't want to waste any time, and Sierra had turned out to be fantastically fertile. They'd conceived right away.

He felt wonderful about it. And terrified, too.

She'd been suffering a lot of morning sickness over the past two or three weeks. Not to mention afternoon sickness and evening sickness as well. He wished medical professionals could get their terminology a little more accurate and honest, and he was worried. Was this normal?

At her first pre-natal check-up, for which their top-flight obstetrician was now running late, not Ty himself, he planned to find out.

A few minutes later, they were called in, while Mayor Taylor chose to remain in the waiting area with the magazines. Ty sweated through a long list of routine questions from the nurse. He asked her about the morning sickness and she said some women could get hit by it pretty bad, but that wasn't a good enough answer to satisfy his doubts.

Then she left, and the obstetrician came in. He did an exam and asked more questions and agreed with his nurse, in response to Ty's question, that, yes, morning sickness could hit some women pretty bad…

…Although sometimes there could be underlying causes for it that needed investigation, he added.

Which was exactly what Ty had feared, and what he hadn't needed to hear.

Sierra seemed quite calm. Lying on the examining table, she smiled at him and his chest started to hurt. He held her hand tighter, as the doctor dimmed the lights in the room and squeezed a clear gel onto her lower stomach for her routine sonogram. He wanted to kiss her so much that his mouth stung.

"This should reassure you," Dr Sandburg said.

He keyed some data into the big machine, then pushed the probe gently against Sierra's stomach. A gray, grainy picture appeared. It was shaped liked the cleared space left in the wake of a car's windscreen wiper and it slid around on the screen in a blur. It made Ty feel queasy as he looked at it, but Sierra was still smiling.

The obstetrician adjusted the probe, and found a small shape. "There," he said. "Beautiful. Nice strong heartbeat."

"That's our baby?" Sierra squeaked.

"It is," the doctor agreed.

Ty couldn't speak.

"Wait a minute, though…" Dr Sandburg frowned, moved the probe again, and watched the screen. Another shape appeared, almost identical to the first. "This may explain the degree of nausea you've been having, Mrs. Garrett."

He focused more intently on the screen, and adjusted the position of the probe so that both shapes were in view at the same time. No doubt about it, there were two.

"Well, how about that!" Dr Sandburg said. He'd lost his serious, professional expression, now, and was grinning from ear to ear. "I guess it's kind of upside-down appropriate, in a way, Mr. Garrett, after all that magazine publicity you had a couple of months ago."

"I guess it is," Ty had to agree. He'd started grinning now, too.

Dr Sandburg moved the probe again, and the two shapes got even clearer. They each had a blurred center, pulsing away in a steady rhythm.

"Oh, wow!" Sierra said. "Oh, *wow!*"

Oh, wow, was right.

Ty could already see the headlines—in the local newspaper, if not in a national magazine. Around seven months from now, the *A-list* Bachelor of the Year and his beautiful wife were going to have twins.

* * * * *

Join Mills & Boon® Tender Romance™
as the doors to the Bella Lucia restaurant
empire are opened!

We bring you…

A family torn apart by secrets, reunited by marriage

There's double the excitement in August 2006!
Meet twins Rebecca and Rachel Valentine

Having the Frenchman's Baby – Rebecca Winters
Coming Home to the Cowboy – Patricia Thayer

Then join Emma Valentine as she gets a
royal welcome in September
The Rebel Prince – Raye Morgan

Take a trip to the Outback and meet Jodie this October
Wanted: Outback Wife – Ally Blake

On cold November nights catch up with
newcomer Daniel Valentine
Married under the Mistletoe – Linda Goodnight

Snuggle up with sexy Jack Valentine over Christmas
Crazy About the Boss – Teresa Southwick

In the New Year join Melissa as she heads off
to a desert kingdom
The Nanny and the Sheikh – Barbara McMahon

And don't miss the thrilling end to the Valentine
saga in February 2007
The Valentine Bride – Liz Fielding

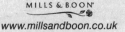

www.millsandboon.co.uk

The child she loves…is his child.

And now he knows…

THE SEVEN YEAR SECRET BY ROZ DENNY FOX

Mallory Forester's daughter needs a transplant. But there's only one person left to turn to – Liddy's father. Mallory hasn't seen Connor in seven years, and now she has to tell him he's a father…with a chance to save his daughter's life!

HIS DADDY'S EYES BY DEBRA SALONEN

Judge Lawrence Bishop spent a weekend in the arms of a sexy stranger two years ago and he's been looking for her ever since. He discovers she's dead, but *her baby son* is living with his aunt, Sara Carsten. Ren does the maths and realises he's got to see pretty Sara, talk to her and go from there…

Look for more *Little Secrets* coming in August!

On sale 7th July 2006

www.millsandboon.co.uk

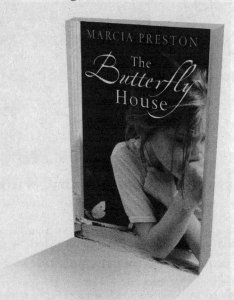

4 FREE

BOOKS AND A SURPRISE GIFT!

We would like to take this opportunity to thank you for reading this Mills & Boon® book by offering you the chance to take FOUR more specially selected titles from the Tender Romance™ series absolutely FREE! We're also making this offer to introduce you to the benefits of the Reader Service™—

- ★ FREE home delivery
- ★ FREE gifts and competitions
- ★ FREE monthly Newsletter
- ★ Exclusive Reader Service offers
- ★ Books available before they're in the shops

Accepting these FREE books and gift places you under no obligation to buy, you may cancel at any time, even after receiving your free shipment. Simply complete your details below and return the entire page to the address below. You don't even need a stamp!

YES! Please send me 4 free Tender Romance books and a surprise gift. I understand that unless you hear from me, I will receive 6 superb new titles every month for just £2.80 each, postage and packing free. I am under no obligation to purchase any books and may cancel my subscription at any time. The free books and gift will be mine to keep in any case.

N6ZED

Ms/Mrs/Miss/Mr ....Initials ....
BLOCK CAPITALS PLEASE

Surname ....

Address ....

....

....Postcode................................

Send this whole page to:
UK: FREEPOST CN81, Croydon, CR9 3WZ